# BREACH

K. I. Lynn

**Breach**

Copyright © K.I. Lynn

Cover image licensed by 123rf.com/ ©sirylok
Cover design by L.J. Anderson

Editors

Chanse Lowell

N Isabelle Blanco

DJ Beck

Publication Date: April 24, 2013

Genre: FICTION/Romance/Erotica

EAN-13: 978-0615789682

ISBN-10: 0615789684

Library of Congress Control Number: 2013905655

Copyright © 2013 K. I. Lynn

# ACKNOWLEDGEMENTS

Special thanks to:

My husband, David, for his support and encouragement in my writing endeavors. Crystal, for without her friendship, support, and guidance I would never have entered this journey. Massy, for being the voice of wisdom and clarity. Stephanie, for sharing is caring. Kyla for her sessions. Nyddi for her unending encouragement and help through this process. Deborah for her support and teachings. Chrisann for her perspective and love of lemons.

Last, but very much not least, to SM for writing a beautiful love story that helped me find the passion in life I was missing, and the fandom for bringing me friends, family and the courage to spread my wings.

Words can never express my gratitude and love to you all.

# PROLOGUE

Hands.

They were punishing. He grabbed my waist with a feral grip, pulling me to him hard while he thrust into me even harder. The way we both needed it.

There would be bruises in the morning from where his hands found purchase, but I didn't mind.

The day was the same as the one before as he took from my body, my heart, my soul. In return he gave himself to me the only way he knew how: with bruising hands, passionate kisses, and hard thrusts.

His body was sin, his cock was sin, and I was a sinner.

His hands moved up my thighs, his long, slender fingers playing my body, bending me to his will. They were a delicious torture, just as much as his words.

His lips sucked at my neck, teeth digging in, making my eyes roll back; another mark.

I grinned. He loved marking me, and I loved hiding them from people. They were proof, a reminder of his need, his pleasure.

My tongue ran up the column of his neck before I found the perfect location to mark him as well. The spot I choose, just below his ear, would make it visible, unable to be hidden by the collar of his dress shirt.

It would make his admirers mad with wonder when they came around to bug him the next day. I smiled at the thought of them finding out he was breaking the rules every day with me, and not them.

Hollywood had nothing on us. Awards could be given for the lies we told, and the feelings we hid under a mask of hate and indifference.

He pulled my hair, bringing my focus back to him. His teeth scraped my neck. No doubt leaving small pink trails on my skin. He growled. "You're not paying attention to my cock, Lila."

A shiver ran down my spine and my muscles clenched around him, eliciting a rumble deep in his chest. He thrust hard, using long strokes, causing me to scream out in response.

He picked up the pace. "That's it, baby. That's what I like to hear." He was pushing me to the edge again. "Scream for me. I want everyone to hear what I do to you."

My mind was fuzzy, lost in a sea of lust. I obeyed and let go, no longer holding back. My screams echoed around the room, and that trademark smirk of his formed on his perfect features.

His mouth moved down to my breasts where he began licking and nipping. The combination of sensations from his body's assault was too much. His name spilled from my lips on a scream as my back arched off the bed. My hands grabbed his arms; nails digging in as my walls constricted around him.

"Fuck, you feel so damn good when you come around my cock."

I was too far gone to respond, my body going lax after my orgasm. He was still going. Both hands were back on my hips as he drove into me. His stamina was unparalleled. How many times in the past had I been forced to come multiple times before he spilled inside me?

"God, I'm close," he grunted before pulling out.

I whimpered at the loss, but knew what he was doing. What he wanted from me.

I managed to turn my body around, coming face to face with his cock and took him into my eager mouth. I lapped up my juices from him as my tongue swirled around his length. His eyes were on me, watching his cock disappear between my lips. He loved to watch me suck him after being buried in my pussy. I sucked hard, punishing him as he had me. I was rewarded with a hiss and a flex of his hips. My teeth grazed his skin. He moaned deep in his chest, his panting gaining speed, muscles tensing.

His hands wrapped up in my hair just as he began to thrust, fucking my mouth. He was grunting and moaning as he hit the back of my throat. I reached up to massage his balls, adding to the sensations.

"Fuck!" he cried out. His hips flexed forward before jerking. He came hard; spurt after spurt, sliding into my mouth and down my throat.

After licking him clean, I released him from my mouth. I smiled up at him and he leaned down to kiss me. The kiss was passionate, as were all his kisses. It was also harsh; his teeth biting on my lip, scraping it, tasting himself.

He got a rag to clean me up before we laid down and curled into one another. Tomorrow was closing in. Another day of wearing masks and hiding what we wanted, what we were, from the world. Another day of denying each other. Another night of punishment to look forward to.

Why was he punishing me? Because I called to him, and I let him do whatever he wanted to me. Punishing himself for wanting me and doing whatever he desired to me.

Punishing us for our breach.

# CHAPTER 1

I t started out as one hell of a morning, so of course it had to be a Monday. It didn't help that I only had three hours of sleep thanks to work keeping me up at night. My brain was unable to shut down. I needed coffee, stat.

The day had to get better—the new hire was starting. Maybe I wouldn't be in the office until midnight almost every night. The prospect of having a life again, thanks to the new employee, was wonderful. Not that I had much of one before. I'd been working seventy to eighty hour weeks for the last four months since Vivian left us high and dry. I needed a vacation.

Hell, I'd settle for leaving before five one evening a week.

I pulled into the parking lot, zipping into my usual spot, and looked into the rearview mirror. My usual bright, expressive eyes were dull and bloodshot from lack of sleep, reflecting dark circles underneath, standing out against my pale skin. My hair was not cooperating, dirty blonde strands sticking up in all directions. I had brushed it before I left, right?

In my current state I wasn't sure of the answer to my internal question. I dug through my purse, locating my hair screws, the most wonderful hair invention ever, and threw the bird's nest up into a quick, tight bun. Looking down, I noticed a run in my hose that started from my knee and ran all the way down my calf.

Great. Add to my already spectacular morning.

I hated wearing pantyhose, but in the winter they helped keep my legs a little warmer when I wore skirts. Surreptitiously, I pulled my skirt up to my waist. My hips jutted forward, feet braced against the floor. I pulled my pantyhose over my ass, down my hips, and peeled the offending material off my legs. As I settled back down, I gathered the flimsy fabric and threw it into the passenger side seat.

I braced my body again, hips in the air, to pull my knee length skirt back down. When I turned to grab my purse, I was startled to see someone watching me.

Fuck.

The driver in the car next to mine was sitting with his sunglasses on. Yeah, like those were needed with the ninety percent chance of rain we were due to have today. I stared at him for a moment, watching a smirk slide across his face. My skin heated, and I cursed at the blush I knew was blossoming.

I flipped him my middle finger before stepping out of the car. Like I gave a fuck what he thought.

I made my way to the double doors and stepped through, taking the elevator up to my floor, and walked back to my office.

Well, it had been my office alone for the past few months, now it was going to be "our" office in the next hour or so. I groaned at the stack of papers that awaited me. The stack had doubled in size over the weekend.

Didn't anyone take a day off? It was clear they had no idea how long it took to go over and prepare all of their documents.

The bright yellow Post-it-note greeted me as I tried to sit down. It was attached to a file: Vivian's file. Great.

My former partner and office mate was suing my employer, Holloway and Holloway Law. "Termination without notification or provocation" being her case. It was a turn of events we all found quite ironic, seeing as she was the one who left for lunch one day and never returned. Job abandonment was what it constituted. I took it as her final "Screw you, Palmer." She knew I'd be the one having to go through it all.

I groaned. As much as I hated how overworked I was of late, I hated working with her even more in our shared office. It felt cramped when she was around. I could never get away from her annoying behavior or loud voice even if I'd wanted to; thanks to the sheer volume of work we received every day.

I was antsy already as I looked at the piles, still surprised the desks didn't buckle under the strain of all the files. So, I wound my way to the break room and got myself a cup of coffee.

After getting a cup of fresh brewed coffee from the break room, I finished up some paperwork left from Friday. Once completed, I began sorting through the new piles, finding the items that were urgent.

I loved coming to the office early in the morning, before the rush of people. It was quiet, and I could concentrate on my work without disruption.

I was halfway through the stack of files when a knock on the door drew my attention away.

"Delilah, do you have a moment?" Jack Holloway's familiar voice called from the doorway.

"For you, sir? Always," I replied with a genuine smile. My boss, Mr. Holloway, or Jack, depending on the occasion – was always kind and easy to talk to, making it a pleasure to give him whatever he wanted. I knew it was because I craved his kind, gentle words; ones that were rarely offered to me by anyone else.

"I wanted to introduce you to your new roommate before the announcement was made." He stepped aside and let a man pass him.

My mouth dropped open at the tall god-like man with light brown hair and seductive blue eyes that stood before me. I sat in stunned silence, eyes wide. Was Jack serious or had my brain shut down?

"This is Nathan Thorne; he'll need your guidance until he's acclimated to how we operate. Please take good care of him."

"Delilah, was it?" the God asked with a smirk. A smirk!

He held out his hand, and with reluctance, I slipped mine into it. We shook for a brief moment before Mr. Holloway toted him away for a chat before the big office reveal.

I remained in silence while my still coffee-addled brain processed the newcomer.

Then it hit me.

*Shit!*

It was the guy from the parking lot. The sunglasses-wearing moron.

I could already tell he was going to be trouble; he was way too good looking, and all the women would be falling over themselves to get to him…in our office.

4

Perhaps Vivian wasn't that bad after all.

My attention returned to the endless piles in front of me, and I resumed working. It wasn't until after lunch that Nathan came back. I spent the next hour helping him get set up; time I didn't have to give. It was a bad idea, the monumental kind, to be that close to him.

We weren't very far in, when the innuendos began and my patience started to wear thin.

I leaned over him to guide the mouse where I needed it. "Okay, so here's the path to the shared drive. All documents have to be saved out on this drive for backup purposes."

"You know, you don't have to climb all over me to get my attention. Lifting your skirt works very well," he said.

My blood was on fire, even more so than it had already been due to annoyance. "Sorry, I didn't realize there were any voyeurs around. Next time, I'll lock myself up in an empty room to spare you." I rolled my eyes before getting back to the task at hand; ready to show him the next step.

"Spare me?" His eyebrow was cocked, a curious look on his face as he took me in.

"Yes, temptation is the road to Hell, or at least that's what I hear." I once again tried to draw his attention back to the computer screen.

He smirked, something I was already beginning to loathe. "You think I'm tempted by you?"

I thought about the answer, though I knew it already, but decided to string him along. "No, but I don't want to *give* you the opportunity to be tempted by me."

"Why so hostile?"

"Look, Nathan," I huffed. "I'm here to do a job, not to flaunt my breasts around to catch your eye. I like my job, I like doing my job, and I want to keep it. Plus, I know you do *not*, and will *not*, be interested in a woman like me, so why even try? Now, can we get back to your tutorial?"

"How do you know?"

My jaw locked, eyes closed before I turned to look at him. "Excuse me?"

"You heard me," he replied. His voice had dropped, now hard and cold, no hint of flirtation. "How. Do. You. Know?"

He was demanding, making the hairs on the back of my neck stand up. My façade was slipping, so much that the words came out as nothing more than a whisper. "Just drop it."

"How?"

"Why would anyone?" I sneered at him before taking off to the restroom.

*Shit, shit, shit!*

I paced the length of the bathroom, taking deep breaths to relax and regain my composure. He'd made me slip, probing me with questions that were best left alone. The answers to those questions brought up emotions best left buried in the past.

After about ten minutes, it seemed safe to exit. When I entered our office, he was staring at me with a perplexed look on his face. He didn't speak, for which I was thankful. I walked back to my desk, bringing my chair around to his, resuming our tutorial.

"Email and contact lists. Then we can see if you have access to the programs IT was supposed to set up over the weekend."

"You're very peculiar, Delilah."

6

"I'm just a woman, Nathan. Nothing special," I replied before focusing back on his computer.

⸺⸺⸺ ⟫⟫⟨◆⟩⟫⟫ ⸺⸺⸺

"Do you have to do that?" My teeth were grinding after almost five minutes of pen clicking from my new office mate. The sound was so loud it was echoing off the walls, distracting me from the contract in front of me.

Nathan continued his assault on the pen's button. "It's my thinking tool."

I glared at him. "Well, your thinking tool has me thinking about all the ways I could harm you with it."

He stared back at me, defying my request and clicking it again. "That time of the month, Palmer?"

"You're an asshole. Get back to work." I forced my attention back down to the papers in front of me.

"Which leads me to the question: what have you been doing for the past four months?"

Death wish. He had one.

I knew the blood vessel on my forehead had to be protruding from the annoyance and anger he was eliciting. It had been three days since he began, and Vivian was looking like a ray of sunshine compared to him. I swear he was trying to get under my skin, provoking me. I just wanted to know why.

"Hi, guys!" A feminine voice called from the door.

I wanted to scream.

Women had been coming in all week to "introduce" themselves to Nathan. The amount of cleavage I'd seen that week alone was

7

more than I'd seen in the entirety of my life, and I had breasts. They all had me wondering if every woman in the office bought a whole new wardrobe full of low neck collars the night after he started.

I was also about ready to snap. Nothing was getting accomplished with their constant interruptions.

I watched for a moment as Kelly flirted with him. My nose wrinkled in distaste, wondering if I'd ever be able to tolerate him, and if he'd ever stop baiting me.

He was a good lawyer, but it didn't excuse his after-hours activities presenting themselves in my office during business hours.

He was hot; there was no denying that. I could agree with them there. I was a single, straight woman, not blind, deaf, and dumb.

Nathan smiled at Kelly. "What can I do for you?"

My hand was resting on my stapler. I resisted the strong urge to chuck it at his head while I stared him down.

He was encouraging them, causing me to want to strangle him. There was a witness, and I valued my freedom, so that plan was a no-go. If I was going to take him out, it wouldn't be at the office. Maybe some dark alley late at night, where I wouldn't get blood all over my desk.

With my annoyance at its limit, I got up and headed out, leaving what was bound to be a peep show. I was almost running as I muttered about refilling my coffee.

Upon entering the break room, I heaved a sigh at the sight of the empty coffee pot. Oh well, it meant fresh coffee for me and more time away from him.

"Hi, Lila! How are things going with Nathan today?" Caroline, my one friend and ally, asked in a teasing tone. I'd told her all about the situation with the asshole. The smile on her face faltered when she saw my expression. "Homicide is *not* an option."

I couldn't help but chuckle at her dead-on comment. "Are you sure about that, Carrie?"

"Yes. The Boob-Squad still coming around?"

"Boob-Squad member number seven is in my office as we speak." I plastered a fake smile on my face, attempting the best impersonation of them I could muster.

Boob-Squad was the name Caroline had bestowed upon all the women who now seemed to have a route past our – my and Nathan's – office.

She attempted to reassure me. "I'm sure it'll get better. Everything has an adjustment period, right?"

I laughed at her optimism. "Sure, why not? Maybe hell will freeze over as well?"

I watched the coffee pot fill up, and pulled it from the burner before it finished. I wished her a good afternoon with my now full cup in hand, and turned to head back. As I left, she begged me not to end up in jail, but I couldn't make her any promises.

When I returned, Boob-Squad number seven was nowhere to be found, and I let out a sigh of relief.

"Which girl do you have your sights set on?" I took my seat, caffeine injection number five for the day in hand.

"Excuse me?"

"Which one? They've all been vying for your attention; wondering which one of them you'll pick to screw first. I'm amazed they're throwing themselves at you, not even caring about their jobs."

"You're talking about the non-fraternization policy."

"Holloway is very strict on it now, ever since the Antonio and Karen incident. Lots of drama and problems there as a result. So, now they get rid of one or both parties. That's why it surprises me so many of them are willing to give up their jobs for your junk."

His face lit up with that smirk which made me – and every other woman in the office – wet. "I do have pretty impressive junk."

I snorted, rolling my eyes. "*Please.*"

"Do I need to prove it to you?" He stood, hands at his belt buckle, pulling the leather through the first loop.

I hid my eyes behind my hand. "Keep it in your pants, Casanova."

"I'm surprised you care about them."

"I don't."

"Then don't worry. One of the reasons I agreed to come here was because of their strict enforcement of no office fraternization. I thought it would keep them away, but it doesn't seem to be enough." He sighed, his expression becoming dark; turbulent.

"Do you want me to throw you a pity party because women are throwing themselves at you?"

My eyes widened at the look on his face. His eyes were now dead, holding none of the light and humor they did a moment before. The smile fell from my face. The arrogant look I'd been viewing over the last few days was gone. His playful glint replaced with tortured darkness. My jaw slackened as the atmosphere changed.

"They should all stay away from me." His voice was barely above a whisper as he spoke, right before getting up and leaving.

I couldn't help but stare after him for a few moments before my gaze moved back to the work in front of me. A shiver ran through me as realization dawned.

There was much more to Nathan Thorne than what appeared on the polished surface.

# CHAPTER 2

I spent the following weeks trying to work out the enigma that was Nathan Thorne, to no avail. After his mood altering comments, he had escaped, returning some time later as the man I'd known up to that point. With careful glances, I watched the way he interacted with others, but there was no hint of the pain I'd seen in his beautiful features.

Whatever plagued him was hidden well under his charismatic personality and good looks. The one glimpse I'd been privy to, kept me up at night. What an odd thing for a man like him to say.

I should've been more concerned with the fact that I was losing sleep over a man I couldn't get along with – something I couldn't afford as I already didn't sleep much – and he'd become the star in all of my fantasies.

"Morning," I said with a yawn as I trudged in on Friday, the end of Nathan's third week with Holloway and Holloway.

Not that I was counting.

"Coffee?" he asked, holding a cup toward me.

I eyed the cup before glaring at him. "Is it poisonous?"

He chuckled, the sound making wetness pool between my thighs. Stupid body, reacting to a man I couldn't stand.

"No, Delilah. Fresh brewed."

"Are you buttering me up for something?" I inquired before taking the cup from him.

"No. I saw you walking in when I was heading to get a cup of my own. With as much as you drink, I figured you'd need one."

"Oh." I was stunned he would do something nice for me. "Sorry… Thank you."

I smiled at him, half-genuine and half-rehearsed. His face lit up for a fraction of a second before turning to a grimace.

"Don't mention it." His gaze returned to his desk and the papers that adorned it.

There it was: that faint glimpse. He stopped himself from what could've been a real smile, for reasons only known to him. What was it that had me so curious about him, that with each new insight revealed, I was left breathless wanting to know more?

———— ⟫⟫⬤⟪⟪ ————

I called it quits about six that evening, ready for the weekend. It'd been a long frustrating week, and I was in desperate need of a drink to unwind. There was a bar within walking distance of

13

my condo, one I'd been frequenting every weekend over the last few months.

"Hey, Lila!" John, the bartender, greeted as I entered.

"Hey, John!"

"Usual to start?"

I nodded, and he got to work on my shot and Long Island Ice Tea.

Not only did I need it to unwind, but it would also help me get some sleep.

"Tough week?" He handed me the shot before making my other drink. "Insomnia still got you?"

I tipped back the rum, cringing against the strength. "Yup. I feel like my brain should've melted at this point."

"Holloway got you any help yet?"

"Yeah, he started a few weeks back, but he's kind of a jackass."

He gave a sympathetic frown. "That sucks. He at least good-looking?"

I eyed John for a moment, wondering if I was in some sort of set up. "Yes, he is. Fuck hot and has every woman in the office chasing him around, hoping he'll break and, I don't know, just drop trou right there and plow into them."

He snickered, handing me the Long Island. "Every woman but you?"

"What's the point?" I shrugged. "First, he's an ass. Second, he wouldn't have any interest in me anyway, so why bother making an idiot of myself?"

"Honey, you are beautiful and sexy. I wish you could see that for yourself. You get my regulars all riled up when you come in here."

"Yeah, well..." I trailed off. There was no response to give.

14

John left to tend to some other customers, leaving me sipping on my drink and contemplating a game on the TV screen in front of me. The sound of the door opening wasn't uncommon, but the shiver that ran down my spine was not normal.

"Can I get a Dos Equis?" The newcomer asked.

I didn't need to turn to know who it was, nor to know he was looking at me. I was too tired and too tipsy to care.

"Palmer?" I knew he was smirking, just by the tone he used. Jesus, I couldn't deal with him tonight.

Could I not think about him for five minutes? He had to be a drunken illusion, even though I'd had little to drink. There was no reason why he would be at my local dive bar.

I tilted my head toward him, his reliable smirk the first thing to greet me. Okay, not an illusion. "*Thorne.*"

He brushed off my attitude. "What brings you here?"

"I'm here every Friday. Why are *you* here?"

"I needed a drink. I just spent the last hour trying to lose Kelly. I think she was trying to find out where I live."

"And of course you had to land in my bar." I huffed.

"Does it have your name on it?"

"Here you go," John interrupted, setting a bottle down in front of Nathan. "Wanna keep a tab?"

"Sounds good."

John smiled at me. "Lila, you good?"

Crap. He was going to give me shit about Nathan the next time I was in.

"One more."

John nodded and went to make my second Long Island, leaving me once again with the asshole.

"*Lila?*" Nathan leaned his arm against the bar.

15

"Short for Delilah." My tone was clipped.

"I've never heard anyone call you that nickname."

"Only Caroline at the office does. Delilah is more professional, so only my friends call me Lila." I hoped that would be enough to sate his curiosity.

It seemed to, because that was where the conversation stopped. I was not in the mood to talk. All I wanted to do was drink, then crash. I was exhausted, and tired to the point of tears.

Sleep called to me; the need to shut out the world and turn off my brain. He made no move to speak as we sat next to one another. The feeling that we were in the same boat came over me as we stared at the screen in front of us. There seemed to be a weird tingling, an almost buzzing sensation, crossing between us. I wondered if he felt it too, or if my tipsy brain was imagining it.

An hour later – after I downed my second Long Island – I was ready to go home. I paid my tab, said goodnight to John, and told Nathan I'd see him on Monday, before I stepped out into the cold early-March air.

After I had walked a couple of blocks, I noticed the sound of footsteps following me. I turned to find Nathan about thirty feet behind me.

"Are you stalking me now, Thorne?" I turned back around before I became dizzy, fell down, and embarrassed myself.

"You wish, Palmer. I'm headed home myself, and making sure you get home all right in your drunken state. Last thing I need is to be implicated because your drunk ass was last seen with me before you disappeared or wound up dead."

"I can take care of myself; don't worry your pretty little head." I walked up to the door of the fifteen story luxury condo building I lived in. "Well, I'm home, so off you go."

He followed me in anyway, and I lucked out that an elevator was waiting in the lobby. I waved hello to Mike, the night guard, and walked in. When I turned to press the button, Nathan was entering as well.

"Seriously, Thorne, you can go home now."

He chuckled before leaning in to whisper in my ear. "I *am* going home."

His statement hit my brain at the same time his scent did, and I staggered back. The man was the most powerful walking aphrodisiac.

His hand shot out to grab my arm, steadying me. I gasped at the contact; electric tingles coursed through, where his hand was and turned to fire between my legs when his grip tightened. I groaned to cover up my slip, but it might have come out as a moan instead.

"Do you really live here?" I whined, pleading to God that it wouldn't be true.

"Fourteenth floor."

The floor just below the top penthouse held not two, like most floors, but one large condo. Four bedrooms, four baths, much larger wrap around veranda, and way out of my price range.

"You're telling me I can never get away from you?"

"What, you think because we live in the same building I'm going to come find you? Dream on, Palmer, you're not that pretty."

I flinched at his words, an involuntary reaction I'd never gotten over. I tried to keep the words from repeating, from drawing up others like it, but it was futile.

"I know that, asshole."

He chuckled, and then stopped once the words processed; his eyes wide. "Wait... What? You're agreeing with me?"

"Of course I am. I'm not stupid," I said, the words screaming in my mind. "I know I'm plain, boring and a workaholic... useless."

I slapped my hand over my mouth. My drunken brain was revealing things I never wanted anyone to know, least of all him.

But the words remained. Repeating over and over like a broken record, until it was taking everything I had to keep them down. I was stronger than them.

"Lila?" he questioned.

I wasn't so drunk that I didn't notice the use of my nickname.

"Sorry, I'm a depressed drunk." I plastered a fake smile on my face. The elevator pinged, alerting me we'd arrived on the eleventh floor. "Have a good weekend."

I waved, but didn't give him time to respond or talk about my rant. I made my way down the hall and into my condo, flicking lights on as I moved through to my bedroom and to the bathroom. Standing at the mirror, I stared into a copy of the unique grey-green eyes that haunted me, and repeated my mantra, the one that always brought me back. It calmed me, but the memories started trickling through the cracks Nathan had unknowingly created.

I sank down to my knees, my fingers gripping the sink as I tried to glue the fissures back in place.

It was apparent Nathan could be my undoing.

18

It was midway through the next week, and it had been a long day. I was exhausted since I hadn't slept much the last few nights, and we were still in the office working, even though it was almost ten in the evening. I struggled to keep hold of my verbal filter since my patience was almost non-existent at that point.

My eyes shifted over to him, and he was still reading the same document he'd been studying for the last half hour. My blood boiled, pumping through my body like a freight train.

"Jesus-fucking-Christ, Nathan!" I yelled in frustration at his slowed pace. "I would like to leave some time this century."

His gaze snapped up and met mine, his eyes in slits. "Well, I do believe this is your fucking fault for telling Jack we could have all of these contracts done by Friday morning!"

"Yes, well, it wasn't a fucking problem until you told Jennifer we would have her contracts for the Sampson takeover ready by Thursday!"

Jennifer Akins, aka Boob-Squad member number one, was president of the Nathan Thorne fan club. She came around flaunting her chest in front of him every single day, at any opportunity she could find. There were now twelve official members of his fan club, so Jennifer wasn't the only distraction during the day, as each one of them filed in at some point.

"If you had informed me of your agreement with Jack, we wouldn't still be here."

"If you read your fucking email, you would have known."

"You're saying *fuck* a lot tonight, Delilah. Something on your mind?" He raised an eyebrow at me.

"Get your mind out of the fu—just get moving so we can leave, okay?"

He smirked at my slip, a look I'd become accustomed to because he loved to taunt me at every opportunity. I was surprised to watch his lips morph into a lazy smile, his tongue peeking out to wet his bottom lip. My gaze zeroed in as it glided over those perfect lips. The man was sex on a stick, and he knew it.

I eyed him sideways, trying not to give myself away. Sometime earlier in the evening, he'd taken his suit jacket off, loosened his tie, popped open the top buttons of his shirt, and rolled up his sleeves. Why did he have to look that *fucking* good while sitting a few feet from me?

"With all the times you've said 'fuck' tonight, I think I know what you really want. What you need, *Lila*."

"What is it that you think I *need*?" I was getting more pissed off, and, to my annoyance, aroused at the same time.

"Cock. You need a fucking hard cock in your tight little pussy." He let out a ragged breath, eyes dilated.

My jaw dropped as I looked at him in disbelief. He was just playing with me, he had to be.

I quirked a brow at him, trying to portray calm and aloof, when inside I was tugging at my hair and fanning my face. "You're an expert on what my pussy needs?"

His eyes darkened as they looked me over, his fingers flexing in what appeared to be agitation on his desk. "Yes, and it needs a cock to fuck it."

"What makes you think this?" I tried to keep my voice steady, but it wasn't working. He was right, and his words were turning me on as much as the growing look of lust in his eyes.

"I can tell."

"Well, fucking finish so I can go home and get off with my B.O.B. He might not be flesh and blood, but he gets the job done."

His eyes darkened and I knew the vision of me pushing a vibrator in and out of my pussy was playing in his mind.

A moment later, there was no desk between us. In a split second, we'd gone from arguing, to his body pushing mine against the wall. His hands pinned my arms to the hard surface, a shuddered breath leaving his chest.

I licked my lips, my body lighting up at his aggressive display. My body was on fire. I couldn't think; speak. How was he doing it to me?

He leaned in, his face next to mine, lips tracing the shell of my ear as he whispered, "Does that turn you on?"

I resisted the urge to turn my head and find his lips. I wanted to feel them against mine, to taste him. There were many ways I wanted to taste him, but that was the first. My body betrayed my need, bowing into his.

"My, aren't you a naughty girl, panting for it. Tell me, Delilah, are you a dirty whore that likes to be fucked?"

He was a dirty-talker—I was screwed. I'd always fantasized about being with a dirty-talking man, and now I had one pressed up against me.

His voice was deeper, somewhat rough, making my desire for him grow. It was useless resisting – I wanted him. By his display, I had a feeling he could bring me the pleasure I'd never found with anyone else.

His hips rocked forward, pushing his hard cock into my stomach. My breath caught in my throat, cutting off my words, as my entire body ached for him.

"Answer me." He pulled my arms above my head. "Are you a dirty whore that likes to be fucked?"

I sucked in a ragged breath before whispering, "Yes."

A victorious smile broke out on his face before his lips crashed to mine, his hands released me then, wrapped around my body. It wasn't gentle or sweet. It was passionate, needy, and full of bite. His teeth grabbed my bottom lip, pulling it then diving back in for another bruising kiss. My hands moved into his hair, tugging at his light brown locks. He growled, and I almost came from the sound.

Fulfilling my unspoken words, Nathan's hand moved down to my waist, his fingers kneading the flesh beneath. They relaxed a bit, almost unsure.

"Harder."

His eyes widened at my request, and I realized the word had escaped my lips, revealing my secret need. I didn't have time to blush or attempt to backpedal; he gripped tighter, lifting me from the ground, pressing my back against the wall he'd pinned me to. My legs wrapped around his waist, pulling him close to the apex of my thighs, where I needed him most. His hand moved up, pushing the material of my skirt with it, opening my legs further.

Hard strokes of his hands worked their way up my torso before ripping open my button-up blouse. I was oblivious to the pinging sound of the buttons bouncing off the furniture, due to my own ragged, erratic breath, pounding in my ears, until one of them hit my leg. With a rough hand, he grabbed onto my breasts. He pulled the fabric aside and twisted my nipples between his fingers. I moaned at the feeling, my hips pushing into his.

"You have beautiful breasts. Fucking perfect, perky tits."

Leaning down, he took one of my nipples between his teeth and pulled. His tongue flicked out to tease, his hand mimicking on the other side. I cried out, my body on fire with need for him, shaking with desire.

"Please, Nathan." I needed him inside me, fucking me, taking me.

"Please what, Delilah? I don't know what you want if you don't say it."

He smirked, and I glared at him in return. I didn't want to play his game; I wanted him inside me. My mind screamed out at him, calling him every nasty name I could conjure. His movements ceased, hands no longer moving but resting against my skin.

I gritted my teeth and growled. "Please, take out that big hard cock that I can feel you hiding, and fuck my pussy with it."

"*That* was fucking sexy," he replied, before tearing his shirt open. His hand moved between us, shredding the fabric that had been my panties away. He undid his belt and pants.

Once his cock was free, he rocked his hips, running his hard, silky length against my wet folds, teasing my clit. "Is this what you want?"

"Yes." I whimpered, pushing against him.

His hands returned to my waist as he lined himself up with my entrance. "Then fucking take it."

I cried out as he drove his cock into me. The force of his thrust was hard enough to rattle the painting that hung a few feet away from where we were. There was a brief second of a pause before he pulled out and pushed back in with the same intensity. In two strokes, he had me on the edge, my eyes rolling back as he filled me. I was so drenched for him he slid in and out with ease.

"So deep!" I managed to cry out between pants. My eyes screwed tight as I soaked up the pleasure, my head lolling against the wall. I was no longer able to do anything other than feel his cock pumping into me.

In with a slam, and then out. *Slam!* Out. *Slam.*

His movements were relentless, making me feel him almost to the point that I could take no more. He grabbed onto my jaw, tilting my face down and bringing us almost eye-to-eye.

"Open your eyes. Don't you dare look away," he warned, driving harder.

I cried out softly. "Can't...too much."

"You will. Even when I make you come and you're screaming my name. Or I won't let you."

I whimpered again, and he knew why; there was no denying his words were pushing me closer to orgasm. My muscles tightened, and my eyes threatened to close, my body giving into his assault, shaking as I tipped over the edge. I complied and screamed out his name as I came hard, my eyes never leaving his. The feeling of him continuing to thrust so hard while my walls clenched around him, was severe.

"Good girl. Fuck, that was so fucking hot. You feel so good when you come around my cock." His lips found mine again; another hard kiss.

I couldn't believe he was still going, his hips moving hard and fast. It was heaven and hell wrapped into one. His lips moved down my jaw to my neck, nipping and scraping at the flesh beneath as he went.

He buried his face in the crook of my neck, his mouth continuing its attack. It felt so good when his teeth dug deeper, marking my skin, but not breaking it. Each nip sent a wave of fire pulsing through me, making me wetter for him. The rumble in his chest grew as his hands tightened around my hips, making it pretty obvious he could tell.

I was in sensory overload from his cock, grip, and teeth, not to mention his body pinning me to the wall. Everything he did made me his. With every thrust of his hips, every dirty word, and every bite, he claimed me.

He bit down on the meat of my shoulder, and I screamed as a second orgasm ripped through me. My hands searched for something to grab hold of, and they found his neck, pulling him ever closer as my body shook. A groan escaped him; the rhythm of his hips became erratic as my walls milked him.

I was still coming when his teeth clamped down harder and his hips slammed flush with mine. I could feel his cock pulsating as he spilled inside me, pushing further into me with each spurt.

We were both breathing hard as we came down from our sex-induced high. His knees buckled and we slid down the wall, his forehead resting on mine. After a moment he removed himself from me; my body mourned the loss.

Standing up, he straightened out his clothing as he began pacing. I stayed where I was on the floor, my eyes watching him. My muscles resembled Jell-O too much to move. He gathered up his suit jacket and threw it on, never stopping his pacing. His hands moved through his hair, pulling at his neck, while he whispered "shit" over and over again, so low I almost couldn't hear him.

He was regretting the greatest sex of my life. Fantastic.

He stopped and turned toward me, and my eyes widened at the look of absolute hatred and disgust that met me. His hand grasped the coffee cup on my desk and hurled it into the wall, making me jump. The ceramic shattered into pieces before landing on the floor.

"Fuck!" he screamed, then flung the door open and stormed out.

I was left sitting on the floor, stunned, staring at an empty doorway. After a few minutes, I knew he wasn't returning, and I picked my tired, sore ass up off the ground. I collected my torn and tattered clothing, trying to redress myself as best I could with what I had remaining. With wobbling legs, I gathered my purse and walked out to my car, leaving the office in a state of disarray.

# CHAPTER 3

I t was hard to pull myself from the warm comfort of my bed
the next morning. I ached, and my mind begged to call in
sick. It wasn't going to happen, though.

My hand slammed down on top of my alarm clock, shutting
off the offending piece of plastic. I turned on the light and slid
out of bed.

My feet were dragging as I entered the master bath, rubbing
my tired eyes in an attempt to wake up. I stopped in front of the
mirror and stared at my reflection, shocked at what I saw. My
normal bird's nest of blonde hair and the dark circles from lack
of sleep were present. What wasn't normal were the black and
purple marks that marred my skin. There were hand prints on my
hips from where he'd grabbed me, imprints of his teeth around
my neck and shoulders, and small bruises along my chest.

It was cold out so I could get away with a high collared shirt. I stared at myself for a moment. Was that really what I should've been concerned about? If his teeth marks were visible or not? Shouldn't I have been concerned there were marks at all? I wasn't embarrassed about them, they were a reminder of the pleasure he'd given me. I found I *liked* them. How twisted was I? While turning to step toward the shower, I groaned. My legs felt like they were no longer connected to my hips, and I was in major need of some aspirin for the ache between my thighs. There was no doubt; my pussy was sore from the pounding Nathan's cock had given it. I never did see the glory between his legs, but I sure felt it, and he was well-endowed.

The spray was cold, turning warm after a minute, and I felt myself slipping back into the out-of-body experience I had when I left the office the previous day. I stepped under the warm spray, the water wrapping around my body, loosening my muscles. The moment I started to relax, my eyes snapped open.

Nathan lived in my building.

I'd be seeing him soon if I didn't run into him on my way.

Panic began to rise within me. He'd been so angry when he left. Would he still be? If he was, I didn't know if I could be in the same space as him. It would be too much; I'd crack. I had no idea what to do when I next saw him, nor did I have any idea how he would react upon seeing me.

"Stop it! You're making yourself crazy when there's not a fucking thing you can do about it," I told myself.

I returned to showering, taking several deep breaths to clear my head.

After my shower, I pulled out a short sleeve mock-neck blouse and one of my black pants suits, making sure that all of his marks were covered as I dressed. It worked, and anything else could be hidden by my hair.

I let my hair air-dry like always, brushing through the knots in an effort to make it look presentable. It was stick straight and dirty blonde; not much to work with. I decided that I could get away with throwing it up in a bun if it gave me trouble later.

After grabbing my purse, I headed out, locking the door behind me. I was anxious as I waited for the elevator to arrive, my heart racing. I was afraid when it came he might be on it. My nerves were getting the better of me. I let out the breath I was holding when the doors opened and the cab was empty. My shoulders relaxed, a tension I didn't realize I was holding evaporating.

Fifteen minutes later, I pulled into my normal spot in the parking lot and froze when I saw his car was already there. It felt like I was on trial, heading to receive my sentence when I'd done nothing wrong. Other than inwardly swoon at a gorgeous man and let him take me against a wall, that is.

My heart was hammering against my chest and my hands were shaking as I walked down the hall, the office door in view. I let out a sigh when I found it empty, giving me at least a small moment to compose myself. Scanning the room, I could find no evidence of the previous night's activities, and was shocked to find the remnants of the cup had been removed. No buttons from our shirts that had flown around, the papers all back in their stacks, the painting on the wall straightened.

My face flamed at the memory of him tearing my shirt; one of the most erotic things ever done to me.

A noise from behind startled me. I turned to find a wide-eyed Nathan standing in the doorway. We stayed in place, staring at each other as time seemed to stop. Neither knowing what to say or do. A range of emotions crossed his eyes, so fast it was hard to keep up: fear, anger, sadness, and, the strongest, regret.

Stepping to his right, Nathan moved to sit at his desk, eyes to the ground as he greeted me in an almost whisper. He sat; our interaction was over, and he continued with whatever he'd been working on. I shook my head to clear it from channel Nathan, forcing my body to respond to me, not him, and sat at my desk.

As I placed my purse in the drawer next to me, I caught a glimpse of a stray white button that had been missed. I picked it up, twirling it between my fingers. My focus was trapped on the button, but I could feel him watching me, staring at it himself.

I set it down and turned on my computer. My eyes never left the small piece of plastic, causing the tension in the room to rise. I could feel how high-strung he was, like he was waiting for the explosion or something equivalent to happen. The need to quell his fears and put him at ease was a strange feeling in me. Despite how the previous night ended, it was still a very enjoyable experience.

"Nathan," I said, my voice low. "I like my job. Do you like yours?"

I turned my passive gaze to him. His eyes were trying to read me, but I knew he was smart enough to understand the meaning behind my cryptic words. The tension melted from his shoulders, and I relaxed a bit as well.

"I do."

"Good."

My attention turned back to my computer. We could move on, keep things professional and maintain our dignity along with a defined working relationship.

At least *I* could. I hoped.

Over the next few days the tension did not dissipate like I expected. Every day he would stare at me before slamming something, then his attention would divert back to his work. The way our office was set up caused us to be in one another's peripheral view all day long, making avoiding him impossible.

The Boob-Squad had been intelligent enough to notice he was having a bad week, and so their visits became less frequent and were work related only.

I said nothing. He said nothing. But we would stare.

I wished he would just tell me what he wanted. I wasn't going to tell anyone, if that's what he was upset about. Nor would I ask for a repeat. He'd made it clear that evening with his actions and temperament, it wasn't going to happen again.

I tried to pretend we didn't have sex; I had to. My job would not be lost over a momentary indiscretion.

"What is going on with him this week?" Caroline asked during lunch one day at our favorite bistro.

"I don't know," I lied. I didn't know what his problem was, so it wasn't quite a lie, but I knew what triggered it. "I wish he would get the fuck over it. It's hard enough to work with his ass when he's in a good mood. Though I will say, it's been nice without the Boob-Squad around so much."

"His pissy mood is rolling out of your office; I don't know how you can stand it in there. Maybe he needs to get laid."

I tried not to gag on the bite in my mouth at her words. If I'd been taking a drink, it would have ended up all over her. "With any hope he'll get over it this weekend. I'm surprised Jack hasn't called him up to have a chat."

"He did." She seemed surprised that I didn't know. "He apologized, said it was a personal matter and would work this weekend to put it to rest."

I wondered if I was the only one that sensed a double entendre in his words. I was the one who caused his mood, and I became nervous at what he was going to do to "put it to rest." I didn't want to swim with the fishes. I was certain there were things I wanted to do in my life.

I almost laughed at the absurdities my brain was creating. Caroline would have, if I'd let it escape.

"Speaking of getting laid…" She trailed off with a wink.

"Shelve that conversation."

"Lila."

"I said shelve it!" My tone was harsher than I'd intended. I didn't want to have that conversation with her again. I was tired of her harping on it almost every week, not because I did it just days before. The need to tell her was great. She was the closest person I had in my life, after all. At the same time I wanted to keep it a secret that Nathan Thorne had been with *me* and no one else in the office.

I chastised myself for even thinking it. I shouldn't be proud of that.

Nathan was damaged, not the perfect being they pined after, and I was the only one who knew it. He guarded it so well, kept his façade secure. Even with his temperament that week, no one suspected. Everyone had a bad day or week; they all thought he'd be right as rain the next. I wondered if he'd ever be right. If he'd be able to defeat whatever haunted him, or move past it. Like I was one to talk.

"Earth to Lila," Caroline called, pulling me from my internal musings.

"Sorry. I didn't mean to snap."

She smiled at me and took my hand in hers. "I just want to see you happy, you know. You haven't been happy since…well, since Drew."

I sighed when his name crossed her lips. I missed him, very much.

Drew was always a ray of sunshine in my dreary life. We tried to stay friends, we did, but even the best intentions sometimes fall to the wayside. My increased hours and inability to get together anytime he called only aided in the rift.

Those were the main reasons that caused it, and he couldn't handle the darkness in me sometimes. My self-worth was already at the bottom of the scale, and plummeted further after our break-up. I had nothing to offer anyone, so why would he stick around?

I threw my napkin on top of my food, my appetite gone with the conversation and the souring of my mood.

"I'm sorry; I know he's still a sore spot." She perked up as an idea hit her. "You should come out with us on Friday!"

"Can't."

"Don't you even dare tell me you're busy, because that is shit and you know it."

33

Her tone was startling. Caroline only raised her voice on rare occasion, and when she did, it was directed at her boyfriend, Ian.

"Next week. I promise."

She sighed and gave me a small smile. "I'm holding you to that. I'll drag your ass out if I have to, and I will employ people to help."

My lips quirked up into a small smile at the image of some mob coming to get me with Caroline at the lead. "Cross my heart and hope to die. Better?"

"Better. But I'm not sticking a needle in your eye. That's just gross." She laughed.

I laughed with her, my mood improving.

When we returned from lunch, I found Nathan struggling, squirming to get away from a member of the Boob-Squad and her obvious advances. She was determined to be the one to cheer him up.

He inched his chair away from her. "Kelly, I'm sorry, I need to get back to work."

I smirked at his predicament. I'd hand it to her, she was tenacious.

"Oh, hi, Kelly!" My voice surprised her, and she jumped down from his desk. "Are you here to pick up the contract to take to the Lowry's? I know Amanda Lowry is anxiously awaiting it." My voice was dripping with sickening sweetness as I asserted my position.

"Oh, yes, Miss Palmer." She was blushing as she grabbed the file from my hand on her way out.

"Thank you," Nathan's melodic voice called, drawing my attention away from the fleeing girl.

My body buzzed at his address. He shouldn't have spoken to me like that. I hated how he could affect me; pull me to him, play with me.

"I didn't do it for you. I just can't stand her presence." Then it began again, the staring. His eyes bored into me, and my body heated under his gaze.

"You and me both."

"T.G.I.F, right? You can get a two day reprieve from your fan club." My voice was saturated with more venom than I'd intended.

He blinked at me, his expression going blank again before turning back to his computer, whispering, "I wish everyday was a reprieve."

Once again, a small speck was given, leading to more questions with no answers.

The rest of the afternoon passed in calm, silent reigning in the office. I ignored Nathan, with the exception of when the two visitors from the Nathan Thorne fan club stopped by. He declined every invitation to go out that evening, citing a previous engagement, leaving them with a promise of a rain check. It seemed to be the only way he could shake them.

I left without much notice a short time later and headed home. Once there, I changed into my jeans, throwing on a tank top and cardigan. I inspected the marks that were fading from my skin. The ones on my chest were gone, but some of the deeper ones on my neck and shoulder remained. On my way, I pulled a scarf off the hall tree and wrapped it around myself, covering the rest.

Being that is was Friday, I headed out to my local dive bar and drank myself into a stupor, despite John's protest. I needed the escape. There was no Nathan to walk me home, but I

35

managed to stumble my way home just fine by myself, as I did every week before he'd showed up. In my drunkenness, I almost hit the button for the fourteenth floor just to show him I could get home fine without him. But then I realized how stupid that would make me seem, and the last thing I wanted to do was give him something more to judge about me.

With only twenty six total units, it was a wonder I'd never bumped into him prior to that Friday night. It was a thought for a less liquored mind, and I stumbled into bed, my brain shutting down as I passed out into the darkness I craved.

# CHAPTER 4

S unday fell upon me before I knew it, and I found myself at home, cleaning an already spotless home. I'd lost most of Saturday to a glorious, deep sleep, waking up just after noon.

Now, I was dancing around to the radio in my tank top and some lounge pants, my hair up in a messy bun. It was unusual for me to leave the house on Sundays, but when I did, I was often dressed in something similar; I needed to feel comfortable after being in a suit all week.

The sun was shining, and I contemplated taking a walk, maybe down to the circle, as it was a warm day. Perhaps I'd stop at the coffee shop or head over to the mall for a movie. Then again, I could always find something on the movie channels, maybe make some popcorn.

A loud, incessant fist, pounding on my front door, startled me, and I ran to answer it. I released the deadbolt and pulled open the door to find Nathan, standing in my doorway, his expression wild.

"Why didn't you say anything?" he asked as soon as he saw me, his hands braced on the door frame.

"Nathan?"

"Why?"

The pinging of the elevator signaled my neighbor was coming up, and I grabbed onto Nathan's tie, dragging him in. "Idiot! Do you want the whole building to know?"

He ignored my question and began pacing. "I don't get you. All week long I've been waiting for Jack to pull me into his office and fire me, or the police to come, knocking down my door to take me away, and…nothing."

"Why the police?"

He stopped, staring at me, his hand fisting in his hair in agitation. "I practically fucking raped you, Delilah."

My eyes widened in surprise as I stared at him. "Is that what you think happened?"

"Yes!" he yelled. "I took you against your will against a wall. Fuck!" His eyes were roaming over me, taking in the expanse of skin I'd kept hidden from him all week. He swallowed hard.

"Listen, Nathan, I think we need to get some things straightened out, because I thought you understood. First off, I asked for everything you gave me."

"Fuck, you sound like a battered housewife."

I rolled my eyes at him just before my temper snapped. "Will you shut the fuck up? I'm trying to talk!" He stared at me in shock as I resumed. "I'm pretty sure I recall begging you more than once, and I never asked you to stop or said no, did I?"

His hand cupped the back of his neck, and I could tell he was thinking back to that night. There was movement in his pants, and his eyes glazed over.

"No," he conceded and resumed pacing.

"Second, that was the best sex I've ever had in my life."

His agitated movements stopped and his lip twitched. "Really?" His telltale smirk returned for the first time in a week, then turned to a look of despair as a realization hit him. "Fuck, I came inside you."

"Are you clean?"

"Yes."

"Then we're good. I'm on birth control. Third, if I did do any of those things you said, there would never be the possibility you would ever do them to me again...not that you would."

He stared at me, unblinking. "Okay, I'm intrigued. Why wouldn't I?"

"Because no one wants me, so why would you?"

"You have such a fucking low opinion of yourself it pisses me off." His blue eyes blazed, surprising me.

"What?"

"You are so fucking sexy, Lila, that all I can think of doing right now is bending you over that table and slamming into you again and again. Hard. My cock is like fucking steel at the thought of being inside you again. You need to be punished for making me want you this much."

With a wicked glint in his eyes, his gaze roamed over my body, making my pussy twitch at the thought. I stared back at him in disbelief. Once again, words foreign to me were falling from his lips. He took a few menacing steps toward me, much like a predator, and I drew in a ragged breath. My body was heating up and high on the anticipation of what he would do to me. I wanted him to lay claim to me again, mark me.

"Fuck!" he yelled, breaking our trance and pacing again. "What the fuck is it about you?"

Nathan turned to face me. His tortured expression indicating his mood was shifting, once again. I never knew what to expect from him.

"I. Don't. Want. You." He spat as he accentuated each word. I cringed as his harsh words forced open cracks. "And you really don't want me. No one should want me. I'm not a fucking catch, I'm a fucking…"

His fist pulled back as if he was going to punch something, but I lunged out and grabbed it, then with all my strength, pushed him against the wall.

He was stunned, staring down at me with wide eyes. My lips were inches from his, taunting him, playing him back. His expression was one of wariness.

"You think you forced yourself on me? Well, how about a little payback then?"

I dropped down to my knees in front of him and began undoing his pants, driven by the growing need to have him again.

"Shit!" he exclaimed as I pulled his hard cock from its confines. His hands slapped against the wall, palms flat, bracing himself.

His legs were locked in preparation for my mouth. I looked up and found his gaze focused down on me, unblinking and lust filled. His eyes were wide from the anticipation of what I was going to do to him. He was long, thick, and deliciously hard. My pussy gushed at the vision of perfection before me, and I leaned forward, wrapping my lips around the leaking head before taking in as much of him as I was able.

"Fuck, fuck!" His hands moved from the wall and fisted in my hair.

I attempted to work him all the way in, but it didn't happen and was going to take further practice. My tongue pressed against the vein on the underside of his cock as I moved back up, sucking on the tip.

The action triggered the dirty words I'd gotten a peek of. He had no idea how much they turned me on. I loved it.

"Shit, that's it, baby. Fuck, you are such a good little cock sucker."

My head bobbed up and down his length, and he watched with rapt attention; eyes dark, and hooded. I moaned around him, the sensation causing his lips to part in ecstasy.

"You can't stop yourself from craving my dick, can you? It's all you can think about, isn't it?"

His hips began to rock, pushing him deeper, almost all the way in. His hands in my hair began to push and pull me up and down his length so he could fuck my mouth. My panties were drenched.

"You have such a hot, wet, little mouth." He groaned and then slowed his movements as he tried to push my head down, taking my mouth all the way to the base. I choked around him, the intrusion foreign. His sexual aggression was sparking something inside me that had been festering for a long time. "Fuck, I'm all the way in…feels so damn good. You love it, don't you? You love sucking me off like a little cock slut."

He pulled me off him, picked me up, and slammed me against the wall, lips crashing to mine. His eyes were even darker, lost in the lust that surrounded us. "I don't think I want you to swallow me tonight. I want to come in that fucking tight cunt of yours."

He kissed me again, hard and needy. One hand was still tangled in my hair, the other grabbing my ass so hard I anticipated a hand print bruise in the morning.

"How do you taste on my lips?" I asked him in the brief moment his left mine.

He growled, pulling my hips to his, rubbing the fabric of my pants against his very erect cock. "Oh, baby, I'm about to ask you the same thing," he whispered in my ear before biting just beneath.

His mouth worked its way down my neck; tongue licking, teeth nipping. He stopped, his gaze locked on the still prominent mark on my shoulder that had not faded. His finger traced the outline his teeth had created, his tongue mirroring the path before his teeth clamped down.

"That is so fucking sexy." He yanked down the strap of my tank top, exposing my breast.

My nipples tightened against the cool air. Nathan dove down, taking one into his mouth and biting. I cried out in pain and pleasure, repeating the sound when he moved to the other side. He rounded back, sucking hard on the first nipple as his tongue flicked the harden flesh.

He worked his way back up, lips mashing into mine, bruising; our tongues dancing. "Now to taste your pussy. I bet you're so fucking sweet." He inhaled and smirked. "I can smell you from here."

"Fuck!" I cried. His words were going to be the death of me. The thought of his mouth on my clit was more than I could handle. I ached for him to touch me; take me.

"Soon, very fucking soon." His hands grabbed onto the waistband of my pants, pulling them and my panties down in one quick tug.

I pulled my tank top the rest of the way off as I stepped out of my pants; his hands on my skin created paths of fire that shot straight into my quivering pussy. His arm hooked underneath one leg, placing it on his shoulder. He licked and nipped his way from my knee to my pussy lips.

"Baby, you are fucking dripping wet for me." His finger swiped my slit, causing my hips to buck and a moan to escape. I looked down in time to watch as he placed that finger into his mouth, licking and sucking my juices. "Mmm, so good. This is what sucking my cock did to you? Dirty girl, so fucking naughty."

His mouth clamped down on my inner thigh, hard enough to leave a mark. Then his mouth latched onto my pussy, licking up my opening before nipping at my clit, and making me moan like a whore. He was relentless in his attack, pulling me hard to his mouth. Screams bounced off the walls, all emanating from me, from what he was doing to my body.

I'd been climbing toward my orgasm with each touch, my body burning with desire. But when he slipped two fingers inside, pumping them, that was what finally threw me over the edge.

"Oh, shit, Nathan! I…I…" My body shook, head tilting back as my orgasm ripped through me. My hands were in his hair, pushing him further into my pussy, riding his face as I spasmed around his fingers.

"You are so fucking hot when you come." He groaned and set my leg back down. His tongue swiped around lips that were shining with my juices. He stood, pressing his body against mine, grinding his cock into me, and guiding my arms above my head.

I stretched up and captured his lips with mine, tasting myself mixed with him. His fingers flexed against my hips.

"Time to fuck that pussy of yours. That's what you want, isn't it? You like being fucked fast and rough, don't you? You want my cock to own your pussy and pound it hard."

I nodded. His grip moved down to my arm, pulling me down the hall. We walked into the dining room, and he pushed me against the ledge of the table, my hips stinging as they hit the hard wood.

"Bend over and hold on," he instructed in my ear, his mouth latching onto the opposite shoulder where his mark was, teeth scraping against my skin as I leaned forward.

My hands searched out the edge, my body vibrating in anticipation, thighs clenching. I gripped down just in time for Nathan to slam into me in one thrust. The motion had me crying out as he filled me.

"So fucking good! So wet…tight…shit, Lila." He pulled out and pushed back in even harder. The table legs scratched against the floor, moving each time his hips slammed against mine. One of his hands released me and twirled around my hair, pulling my head back. The other hand pushed down on the small of my back, pressing me into the wood surface.

My back arched, scalp tingling in both pain and pleasure as I tightened around him due to the new angle.

"That's it, take my fucking cock. You love it, don't you?"

I whimpered as his pace increased to the pounding state I craved. His hand pressing hard against me held a sexual neediness my body wanted, so different from the touches of my past. His want and desire flowed through his skin into mine.

"Answer me! You love my cock in you, don't you, little slut?"

"Yes. Yes! Please fuck me with your...ugh...hard cock... shit...p-pound my naughty pussy." My mind was unable to keep up with the emotions he was driving into me as he pushed me to the edge.

His grip on my hair tightened, making my head and shoulders arch farther up off the table toward him. "Harder. Deeper, oh fuck...so deep inside me. More! Pull me down, take me over...shit. Make me sorry for being so naughty."

I whimpered again, unable to speak anymore. Incoherent sounds were all that came out. I'd never had it like that, so rough. I loved it. He was gritty, demanding, and had a dirty mouth that sent me into overdrive. But his eyes held no disdain, just desire and lust.

"Yes, punish you. Fuck. I don't want this...don't want you. This." *Slam.* "Is." *Slam.* "All." *Slam.* "Your." *Slam.* "Fault!"

I crumbled beneath him, screaming his name as my pussy clenched around his perfect cock.

"That's it, come on my cock. Shit, your pussy feels so good... Milk my cock, baby. Fuck!" His hand released my hair, and I fell back down to the table, exhaustion taking over as I moved toward a second orgasm. He gripped my hips, pulling me back, pushing him deeper. "That's it. Grip it tight like a vice. That's what you do; it's how you torment me. Fucking cock tease."

My whole body shook, tearless sobs taking over as my oversensitive body tingled, and I fell again. His hips jerked, fingers digging into my flesh as he exploded within me. A moment later his movements stopped, the sound of his harsh breath filling the room.

He collapsed on top of me, unable to hold himself up, muscles spent. We were both panting, trying to regain a normal heart rate.

"You should stay away from me, Lila. I'm no good for you." He placed a soft kiss on my shoulder blade with the tenderness of a lover. "Run while you can. Run away from me, and don't look back. I'm not worth your life."

His eerie warning was the last thing I heard before exhaustion took over and my eyelids closed, blacking out the world.

# CHAPTER 5

M y eyes fluttered open, the familiar sight of my bedroom coming into focus through my disoriented mind. Warm, soft light filtered in through the curtains covering the windows, greeting me from my comfortable bed. It took a moment to recall what I'd been doing before I awoke, confused as to why I was asleep in the middle of the afternoon. A twinge in my abdomen when I tried to sit rectified that.

Nathan had been there, inside me. It was better than the last time, the pain and stiffness when I moved was a testament to his visit. He was rough and dirty, and I knew my body was ruined for any other man. No other could make my body sing the way he had during our encounters.

The last words he said surfaced through my addled mind, playing over, looping until it was clear.

*"You should stay away from me, Lila. I'm no good for you. Run while you can. Run away from me and don't look back. I'm not worth your life."*

All I could think of was: *why?* Why wasn't he "worth my life?" If he wasn't a good or even decent person, would he have placed me in my bed before he left? Would he have even come, so aggravated, thinking he'd hurt me? I was tucked under the covers of my bed, cleaned of our actions, with a glass of water on the bedside table; all evidence to the contrary.

Another question was: why me? Each member of the Boob-Squad was throwing themselves at him daily. We weren't friends, nor did we pretend to be. It was a constant butting of heads, sarcastic remarks, biting words and eye rolls, filling our everyday encounters.

With no answers, I forced myself from the bed and threw on some clothes before I plopped in front of the TV, intent on losing myself in whatever movie was on. I was too tired and aching to even contemplate anymore cleaning. In the back of my mind I wondered if Nathan was upstairs doing the same thing. He was so close, yet so very far away.

---

Sunday had long since passed, and now it was nine in the morning on a Wednesday. I hadn't seen Nathan at all outside of work, much to my body's regret. Our usual bickering never faltered, but his mood improved over the weekend like most thought it would. I was the only one privy to the real reason why.

Out of the corner of my eye, I could see him looking at me, staring at me like he was searching for the answer to a question.

He never looked when anyone else would see, just when we were alone; tucked away in our space with a view.

Our office had once been one of the conference rooms for Holloway and Holloway, back when they only took up one floor of the building. When the firm expanded and the load became more than one transactional attorney could handle, Mr. Holloway split it into two, but kept it together. Hence the occupation of such a large room by comparison.

Vivian was hired to work with Trevor to lighten the burden, making it more manageable. When Trevor's wife was relocated, I applied in hopes to be relieved of the grunt work of a newbie. Mr. Holloway hired me straight out of college after I'd interned between my second and third year of law school.

I had no desire for the court room, I never had, but I loved the law. When I looked at Nathan, I saw a courtroom personality. He was much smarter than I was. I envisioned him prosecuting criminals or suing large corporations. Not stuck in a room, meeting with clients a few times a week, and looking over legal jargon until his eyes bled. The job wasn't him. I assumed it was part of his mystery, but I'd never asked, and he wasn't forthcoming with information about himself.

"Delilah?"

I was pulled from whatever contract my eyes had blurred over while I was thinking about him. The man was too distracting for his own good.

"Yes." I sighed and eyed my empty coffee mug. I could use a fresh one.

"Are you okay? You've been staring at the same contract for the last fifteen minutes, your hands hovering over the keys." His lips pulled up into that damn smirk of his, the one that made panties wet on almost every woman he encountered, mine included. His blue eyes sparkled with amusement, and I wondered if he knew I was thinking about him.

"I just need more coffee."

His smirk grew. "Your mind seemed preoccupied, not tired."

Damn him.

"Don't worry, Thorne, you weren't starring in my preoccupation." I knew it was a lie. A bold faced one at that. I'd thought of no one but him in weeks. I wanted to know all of him, but was aware he'd never allow that to happen.

High pitched giggles drew my eyes to the door; another member of the Boob-Squad had arrived. Wasn't it against the dress code to have your breasts hanging out of your top? I was beginning to think Jennifer hadn't read that memo, or the one about fraternization. Who was I to talk? Nathan's cock had been in me more than once and it was bliss.

"Nathan, I was hoping you could help me." Her flirtation was in full force. It was a blinding and gag-worthy performance.

"I'm going to lunch." I grabbed my purse and coat, heading out before I vomited. They really were vile.

There was a small bit of satisfaction in seeing him squirm as I walked out. I'd bailed him out too many times in the past week; he could fend for himself. I hated them interrupting my work, and I was sick of it, not because I was jealous and wanted to scream out that he was mine while I yanked on their hair to drag them off of him. My stomach twisted in a knot as I imagined one of them with their hands all over his cock; their mouths on his hard flesh.

I wound my way around the cubes of the newbies and interns until I reached an open door. Caroline was finishing up a phone conversation, holding up one finger for me to wait.

"Ready?" she asked as she hung up the phone. I nodded and waited as she grabbed her purse.

"Please, I need to get away from them."

"Ah, he's in a better mood, and now they're all over him again."

I sighed, picturing the scene as I left. "I'm not sure you can say Jennifer's shirt is doing its duty today."

"What does he do with all these women trying to climb into his pants?" she asked as we walked to the elevators. With luck, there was one waiting and we hopped on.

"I don't know, but I'm pretty sure he isn't touching any of them." *Because he's touching me.*

"Why do you say that?"

I snorted. "You should see the look on his face, I mean the *real* look. Their tenacity scares him. I've had to save him more than once in the past week."

Her eyebrow arched up as she regarded me, a smile forming on her lips. "You're attracted to him."

I stared at her openmouthed. "I…I… Shit. Of course I am! Have you *seen* him?"

Her grin widened, and she moved to look forward again. "I'm just happy to find out you haven't lost your libido with two years of cobwebs up in there."

I snorted. "Um, thanks?"

"We still on for Friday?" she inquired. I started to open my mouth, but she silenced me. "You promised me. Don't make me call in reinforcements to drag you out."

I threw my hands up in protest. "I'll go. I'll go."

After a quick bite at a bistro down the street, we headed back. While Jennifer was gone, Kelly had taken her place and was pawing all over him. The girl was only nineteen; did she really think she stood a chance?

51

Then again, guys often went for younger girls.

She was all giggles and flirtation, and he was smiling and joking back. I scowled at him for encouraging their behavior. As I sat down, I woke up my computer, placing my purse in the bottom drawer and attempted to get back to work. My irritation was too great, and only grew as their conversation continued. I turned to glare at them and was met with a grin; he was enjoying my torment. The man was so infuriating sometimes. He knew I was pissed and was rubbing it in my face.

"Kelly, have you set up my appointment with the Sanders yet?" I questioned, knowing the small task I'd asked of her was incomplete. I was drawing at anything to get her out and away from him…*us*. We both needed to work.

"Nope," she answered, and then turned back to Nathan.

I cocked my eyebrow at her, attempting my best icy glare. I couldn't see it, since I was looking at her, but I could tell Nathan was staring at me. "I asked you to set that up three hours ago."

"I'll get to it," she said in an annoyed huff and a roll of her eyes.

"Well, I'd say if you have time to sit in here and talk, you have time to make the call you should have made three hours ago." My teeth were clenched at that point, my voice climbing an octave as I restrained myself from yelling at her. Nathan was still staring at me, but not in amusement; he almost seemed annoyed.

"Fine, I'll go do it now." With a huff, she told him she'd be back before bouncing out the door.

"Better not be," I grumbled under my breath. He was still staring, so I turned to meet his gaze. "What? It's your damn fault they're in here all of the time. You could at least *discourage* their advances."

"How is it my fault?"

52

"Your damn pheromones are drawing in the bees and they're pissing me off. You're the best looking man in this office, and they all want you."

"And you don't?"

My face heated when he hinted for the first time at what we'd done. In a fit of embarrassment and nervousness, I chucked my stapler in his direction. Childish, but I didn't know the right social cue for the situation, and I was afraid he would notice my deficiency. The stapler tumbled on the floor, missing him, and breaking apart.

"Back to work," I mumbled.

"Yes, throw shit, Palmer, that's mature," he snapped, his brow furrowed with anger.

"Do you really want me to go there, Thorne? Tell me, do you plan to screw one of them?"

His voice was low and steady as he said, "No."

"Then why do you flirt with them?"

"Because I've found that being friendly makes people more apt to do what you ask without delay or complaint. You catch more bees with honey, Palmer."

"Oh, that's right, I forgot you're the friendliest person in the world." My voice was dripping with sarcasm. "Oh, wait, no…" I leaned forward and whispered so that no one except him could hear me, "You're damaged and hiding behind a fucking mask."

He snarled, leaning in closer. "You have no idea what the hell you're talking about."

He sat back, jaw tight as he focused back on the screen, his demeanor ending all conversation.

# CHAPTER 6

H e was in a foul mood the rest of the afternoon, but once in a while I found him looking at me again. Though I would almost call it a glare at that point. Kelly never made it back to continue her flirting, but she did stop by to tell me when my meeting was scheduled.

It was almost six when I finished up the contract I was working on, and it seemed Nathan was almost done as well. It wasn't worth getting started on another one, so I decided to call it a night, packing up and heading to the elevator. I left him working, without saying goodbye or waiting.

It was just my luck, though, that when I was getting out of my car, his own pulled in three spots down from mine. I refused to acknowledge him as we entered the lobby. My eyes avoided Thorne as I greeted Mike, the night guard, and I stayed as far away as possible as I pushed the button to call for the elevator. The air around us was charged as we waited, making me anxious. The ping alerted us to the arriving elevator and we stepped on together, each hitting the button for our respective floors.

As the doors slid closed, I kept my eyes trained to the front, but in the smooth metal, I saw him lean down toward me. I held my breath.

His mouth stopped an inch from my ear, his voice low and mocking. "Were you jealous?"

I tried to hide how he affected me, but the small, jagged breath I took was a telltale sign. "No," I replied, trying to keep my voice aloof and indifferent.

"You shouldn't be. I don't want them, and I don't want you either." His words stung, even though I knew why he said them: to push me away. "No," he whispered even lower, his fingers reaching out to play with a stray lock of my hair, tortured tones replacing all others. "That's not true, is it? I don't want to want you, but I do. I fucking crave you, but I can't…I can't give in." He stepped closer, and the current that passed between us grew stronger, want taking over every part of me. "Please, Lila, push me away." His body leaned into mine, his lips running along the column of my neck. "Don't let me take you again."

He was so close I could breathe in his intoxicating scent. It made my legs shake and threaten to collapse out from under me. An inch apart was too far; I needed to feel him pressed against me.

"I can't stop you, I want you too much." I turned toward him, my hand resting on his chest. "You've given me a taste, and now I want more. I *need* more."

I lifted my eyes to meet his. The longing I'd heard in his voice melted from his face and turned to anger.

"Fuck." He backed away from me. "No. Don't say that."

I pulled on his tie, bringing his face down to mine, my lips ghosting his. We were so close. "You're like a drug, and I'm going through withdrawal." My tongue snuck out, lapping against his lips. "I need your help."

My hand slid down, grasping his thick cock through his pants. I was being forward, a trait I wasn't used to, but figured it was because I knew he wanted me, and I needed him. He was reacting, his body rocking, pushing him harder into my hand as he released a deep breath, so I kept going. When his head lifted and his eyes met mine, heat rushed through me. His eyes were dark, wild, and clouded with lust, and I knew I was going to get what I wanted.

The elevator pinged, signaling we'd reached my floor. The war that raged within played out on his face. He wanted to follow me, but the part that was pushing me away, kept him inside. The doors started to close, separating us, and his eyes widened before jumping through to join me.

His hands gripped my waist, mouth latching onto my neck, pressing his erection into me as we walked down the hall to my condo. My body was lighting up with each step, the excitement of him soon being inside me, causing a flood in my panties. I was drunk on him.

My fingers fumbled with the lock, unable to get the key in due to the distraction of his chest molding to my backside. With a few more tries, the door unlocked and we stumbled through. I turned and his lips captured mine, walking me back until I was pinned against the wall. My hands wrapped around his shoulders, pulling him closer.

"I want your hands and lips on me. You've kept me waiting long enough, Mr. Thorne."

"Fuck." His teeth nipped at my jaw. "What about my cock?"

"I want it in my pussy where it fucking belongs." I wondered where my assertiveness was coming from. Who was the woman speaking through me?

"I'll fuck you so hard you won't be able to walk." His voice was low and rough. "You make me so hard; you better be ready to work your ass off for my come."

"More," I begged. My hands worked at undoing the buttons on his shirt as his hands moved to my ass, pulling me harder against him and his cock. I whimpered, my head dropping to his chest, panting with my need for him.

He snickered. "Excited, my little whore? Yes, that's what you are, letting me fuck you the way I do. You know that's not good, letting me punish you. My cock wants to be down your throat, inside your pussy, and," he paused, his grip on my ass tightening, "in your ass. You tease me with it every fucking day."

I'd never done anything like that before—the idea was scary to me, but somehow I knew I'd do it…for him.

I was able to get his dress shirt unbuttoned, but when I went to untuck the undershirt, he stopped me, moving my hands further down to his belt instead. Odd, but I didn't ask. As soon as the zipper was down, I slid my hand in and wrapped it around his hot, silky cock. I pumped him a few times before I moved to my knees, lowering his pants as I went. I leaned forward, my tongue peeking out, and licking around the head before taking him into my mouth.

His hips began to move in small thrusts, a groan leaving him. "That's it, take it all. I'll fuck your mouth until I come, and you'll fucking swallow all of it. Do you understand?"

I moaned around him, slipping him out from my lips. "Fuck, you have such a filthy mouth."

"You think you own my cock, don't you?" He slapped the head of his cock against my cheek, running it along my bottom lip. "You don't, little whore. You don't own it, but you *will* take it." He shrugged off his suit jacket, pushing my head back down his length. His fingers unknotted his tie before gripping my hair as his pace picked up.

With a sudden movement, both of his hands were pushing my head down on his shaft. I gagged at the intrusion, causing Nathan to hiss and moan in response.

"Get your ass up here and let me fuck you the way you want it; hard, fast, and dirty. That's what you want, isn't it?" He was taunting me.

I couldn't protest. He was right, it *was* what I wanted. I was caught in his seductive spell, eager for what was to come, for what he was going to give me.

"It's what I want. To stretch you open and have your pussy suck me back in." His fingers moved down my jaw, grasping on to the back of my neck and pulling me, his lips devouring mine.

He proceeded to rid me of my clothes, yanking my shirt off and pushing my panties to the ground.

"Oh, God!" I cried out as he leaned down, his teeth biting onto my cloth covered nipple, sucking it into his mouth.

"Not God, baby…*Nathan*. That's the name you'll be scream-ing when you come." He unclasped my bra, sending it to the floor with the rest of my clothes.

His fingers wrapped around my wrist, leading me into the living room. I stared at him as we walked, noticing he was still wearing his shirt and pants, which he slid down to his knees as he sat down and leaned back. One hand pushed his cock upright, while the other guided me over, steadying me as I straddled his hips.

Once there, his fingers pinched my nipple, then moved down between us, past my clit, and found the moisture that had settled and pooled at my core. A throaty groan ripped through me the instant his finger slipped inside.

"You're so fucking wet," he groaned. "Was this from sucking my cock?" He pulled his fingers from me, then swirled and dragged my dripping juices straight to my puckered anus. A light pressing of his fingers made my eyes widened. "You're so uptight and frigid; I should warm you up and then impale your ass with my cock. Fucking shoot my load up there."

His fingers flitted, dancing around at my opening, and I had never felt so wanton, so dirty. My hips were moving against him, the tip of his cock hitting my clit each time and making me beg for more.

"Maybe I'll paint you white. Fuck. You'd love that, wouldn't you? Have my come all over your body."

"Please. I want everything you want to give me." I should have been ashamed, but there wasn't room for any reaction except pure unadulterated lust and filthy desire for him and his words.

His fingers pushed back up into my pussy, his thumb hooking onto his cock and pressing it against my clit. I leaned forward, one hand braced next to his head as I drew in a shuddering breath.

"That's it, baby, you love my cock deep inside you. You need me to fill you." His eyes were twisted, dark, and so fucking glorious. I was transfixed, and I was hanging on to every word. He was beyond aroused. It seemed it wasn't just about punishment for him anymore; it was about self-medication and numbing his mind, drowning out his ghosts.

One finger slipped out and back, sliding just inside the entrance, tempting me and sucking me into his world. I wanted to be part of it, be part of his soul. He was my God, and I worshipped him.

"Have you ever had a cock up here?" he asked. I shook my head, my body crying out for him to shove his cock inside me. "Don't lie to me, slut."

I shook my head again. "None...j-just a dildo. Now stop teasing me, and fuck me!"

He grinned up at me, licking his lips. "You're a naughty little slut. I'll show you what it feels like to have a cock shoved up there. Soon." He pulled his fingers from me, his weeping cock released and landing back down on his stomach. "That is fucking sexy, the thought of you stuffed everywhere with a vibrator. You love that, don't you?"

"Y–yes," I stammered.

"My cock likes the sound of that, and," his gaze moved down, "so does your pretty little pussy."

I almost cried with joy when he lined up his cock, but screamed out in pleasure when he slammed me down hard as he pushed up, filling me in one swift movement. My hands moved to his chest for support, while his held my hips in a painful grip, almost bone crushing.

"Damn, you feel so fucking good wrapped around me, squeezing me," he groaned, lifting me up and pulling me back down.

"Deeper," I moaned.

60

"Deeper?" He slowed down and kept his cock at my entrance.

"Fucking tease." I let all my weight relax so he was filling me again.

"Nobody tells me how to do this shit." He flipped us over, pounding me into the couch. My head rolled back, my eyes fluttering close. "Yeah, that's it, squeeze me. Take me all the way in. I'm not going to stop until you're coming while screaming how much you fucking love it."

I smirked at him; he was so full of himself in that moment. His heavy hooded eyes watched, transfixed as his cock disappeared into my pussy with each thrust. His jaw was tight and there was a constant look of furious concentration, as if he was driving his demons out of him with each movement.

He growled. "That is a fucking spectacular view. I could watch it all fucking day."

I was buzzing, my muscles tightening, signaling I was close. Nathan must've felt it as well.

"Come on, slut, come all over my cock. Come!"

I screamed out his name, my nails digging into his arms, back arching as I convulsed around him.

His relentless pounding didn't let up as I came down, it increased. Curses flew from his mouth, the slapping sound of skin filling the room. His sexy sighs, his tortured look as he stared at his cock pumping into me, and his declarations of, "Fuck, that's the shit I love," set me on fire.

I loved watching him, knowing that I was the one making him come apart at the seams. *Me*, I was the one. Not Jennifer, Kelly, or Tiffany. Me.

His eyes met mine, and there was an emotion I'd never seen emitting from them. It was strong, and overpowering. He leaned down and captured my lips, his hand wrapped around the back of my neck holding me close.

My head couldn't wrap itself around the enigma that was Nathan Thorne.

He pulled away, his eyes holding mine—fierce, determined and so damn hypnotic. His body was draped over mine, his pace quickening. Teeth scraped against my skin, biting, marking, as the assault from his mouth moved around. Tongue lashing at my skin, while lips caressed the harshness away. He bit down hard on my shoulder, sucking the skin between his teeth, making sure the mark was good and dark. My walls tightened, and I could feel myself on the edge.

"You're going to come." His mouth crushed mine, and forced my lips open. Several sexy sighs escaped him, flowing into me, and I felt his dick twitch. I smiled at the thought of watching him come undone above me.

He picked up my legs and anchored them over his shoulders. He pumped straight into me, his tip hitting the same glorious spot his fingers had earlier.

"Oh, God!"

"Yes, that's it, baby. Take it. Flood your pussy and let it flow out onto my dick. You know you want to." There was a fierce edge to his voice. His erotic words were not empty or void. I knew he meant every single fucking word.

"More," I said, the word coming out unbidden. My mind was foggy, lost in the Nathan-induced haze.

"Shit! Fuck, baby, you're…oh, fucking…clenching so tight…so fucking tight!" he stammered out, pleasure induced incoherency taking over.

His fingers dug into my thighs, shoving them together and with a force I'd never felt before. It fucking ripped me apart and landed me with an orgasm that was akin to an out of body experience.

"Fuck, Nate. Yes!" I screamed louder than I ever had during an orgasm, shuddering breaths and indecipherable moans, falling from my lips.

Every muscle in his body was vibrating, his head tipped back as he started yelling. "Yes! Oh, fuck, baby, fucking you... God, so good!"

His voice shattered, drowning mine out. I felt a sudden emptiness as he pulled out of me. I stared as his hand pumped his cock, the head straining so much it was almost purple. He let out a strangled cry as the first hot stream was released. It landed on my left breast; the following spraying on my stomach. His body convulsed and swayed, hips jerking with each spurt.

"Shit, that is the best fucking sight in the world," he whispered, licking his lips as he stared down at my body. "You look so fucking good covered in me." He moved his cock around, spreading his come around my skin, staring in perverse fascination.

"That was... God, I can't describe it." I was incredulous as I dragged my hands up through my sweat matted hair.

He beamed at me. "I know."

The damn mercurial man in front of me was so happy. He was beaming at me like he adored everything about me. What the hell? Was it due to my earth shattering orgasm and he was pleased he'd done it to me? Or was there something else going on?

"I don't think I'll be able to walk tomorrow. I want Starbucks in the morning, you're buying," I said between pants.

"How about I tell the other ladies I'm gay? Would that be sufficient payment?" He smirked and slowly pushed off of me.

"I'm not some damn call girl, you know."

Before I could smack him or throw something at his smirking face, he was shrugging his pants up his hips and heading for the door.

"Asshole!" I hollered at him from my gelatinous place on the couch.

"You mean 'thank you!'" He snorted and threw open the door, letting it slide closed behind as he disappeared into the hallway.

# CHAPTER 7

B y Friday morning, I was still walking a little on the funny side, my muscles recuperating. With a coffee cup in hand, I was headed to the break room, only to find Caroline filling up her own.

"So, how's it going today?" she asked, pouring the creamer into her cup and stirring.

I rinsed my own cup out in the sink, then poured myself some. "He's such a pain in my ass!" I tried to keep my lips from quirking up into a smile, and present a pissed off demeanor. Inside I was laughing, knowing one day he'd make it true in a literal sense.

I couldn't tell Caroline about that though. Not yet. I still didn't know what we were anyway. She laughed, before going over the evening plans. I was supposed to be out of the building by five to eat dinner before meeting her and some of our co-workers at eight.

I headed home at the promised time and ate while I scoured my closet for something to wear. It'd been so long since I'd gone out for "fun" that it took me some time to dig out any going-out worthy clothing. Suits and business attire had taken over my closet, making it hard to find anything else.

The air still held a chill, so I settled for a jean skirt and large neck sweater that fell off one shoulder. I dug out some knee-high heeled boots for added warmth on my legs. The thought of tights passed through my mind, but I knew Nathan wouldn't like them.

I didn't even know if he was coming, and even if he did, people we worked with were around, so he wouldn't be touching me or dancing with me.

When I arrived at the destination, Caroline and her boy-friend, Ian, were waiting for me at the entrance, and we were able to secure a large half-moon booth for our group.

I'd finished off a shot of rum, and was starting in on a Long Island, when I felt it. Felt *him—his* eyes.

Nathan was there.

"Hey, Nathan, you made it!" Caroline called out.

I jolted, shooting my friend a death glare as we scooted around to make room. I was on the end, making me the one he sat next to, our thighs touching.

"Wouldn't have missed it," he replied with a smile as he greeted the table. He leaned close to me, whispering in my ear and sending heat throughout my body. "Lila."

I smiled at him. "Nate." His eyes flashed and he drew in a quick breath, but he composed himself before anyone noticed. "I'm surprised to see you out."

"Oh, we used to see him here all the time," Ian chimed in. "Been months, dude. We thought you fell off the face of the earth or something. Finally find yourself a steady girl?"

Nathan laughed, but I couldn't find it in me to join in due to the knife twisting in my gut. Of course he would go out to get his kicks. It didn't slip my attention that Ian said he hadn't seen him since before we started having sex, though.

"So, you're a man-whore? Should have known." I downed the rest of the Long Island in front of me. The thought of his hands on some of the skanks I saw around the place made my blood boil. Okay, the thought of his hands on *anyone* other than me did it, but did I expect him to have been a monk before me?

No. It wasn't rational.

"It was just sex, Delilah. Fucking," he mumbled low enough for just me to hear.

I could feel the bile rising in my stomach, my expression slipping, exposing my displeasure.

*That's right, just sex. You don't mean anything to him other than a good fuck.*

I jumped, flinching when I felt a hand on my leg, right above my knee. Nathan's hand gripped tight, his thumb making small circular patterns on my skin, placing a fire in their wake. His scent enveloped my senses as he whispered in my ear, "I don't want them."

He didn't include me in that comment, as he would previously, grouping me along with the rest of his fan club. A step, I supposed, but a step to what? To him fucking me at his whim? If I was being honest with myself, I wanted more. But I would take whatever he would give just to have a part of him.

67

"I need another drink," I said as I turned for Nathan to let me out. His face was hard and unreadable, and his grip on my leg tightened. My heart rate sped up; he always managed to touch me in a way that excited my body and made it rebel.

"Are you sure that's wise?" His gaze moved to the empty glasses in front of me.

"Are you my fucking father? No, I didn't think so. Let me the fuck up so I can get another drink." I was fuming, no doubt about it. He finally relented, and I pushed past him and through the crowd, clamoring for a drink.

Up at the bar, I tried to get the bartender's attention. Tried, but failed.

"Need help, pretty lady?" a slimy voice asked from behind. I could smell the alcohol wafting off him without even turning around. I crooked my head to find a good looking, but drunk as all hell blond man.

"No thanks, I'm fine." I returned back to my task of getting the damn bartender to acknowledge my existence.

"Suit yourself."

After finally getting some attention, I got a Hard Lemonade and headed out to the dance floor where Caroline and Ian were grinding away. I joined in, the booze and the music taking me away from my inhibitions, and I *danced*.

My eyes were closed, hips swaying to the beat. A body pressed up against mine, but not the one I wanted. There was an arm around my waist, a hand at my hip. The touch was foreign, not what I craved, what I needed, but in my inebriation, I let it stay.

He pulled me back into him, and felt his arousal. The hand on my hip worked its way up my waist, skimming the side of my breast.

It was wrong, all wrong. It wasn't *his* hands, *his* body—Nate. That was who I wanted. Nate.

A chill ran down my spine, igniting my body. I didn't even have to open my eyes to know Nathan was there.

"Can I cut in?" His voice was low and menacing. I opened my eyes to find him staring at me, anger vibrating off of him.

"Wait your turn," a drunken voice said from behind me. I tilted my head back to see the blond that had been at the bar. Ew, I was dancing with him?

Nathan snarled. "I'm not asking."

Funny, people snarled at me in the past, but it had always been frightening. Not so with Nathan; he was turning me on.

"Okay, man, shit, take her," blondie said as he backed away and pushed me at Nathan. I crashed into his chest, hands gripping his shirt. I was unable to stop myself from breathing him in.

"What the fuck was that about?" I pushed off him.

Instead of an answer, he grabbed my arm and pulled me from the dance floor. "You're letting strange men put their hands all fucking over you!" His grip tightened.

"What the hell do you care, Thorne? Huh?"

"Because, you are mi—"

"This guy bothering you, Lila?" A familiar voice boomed out over the music, cutting off whatever Nathan was about to say.

My head snapped to the side to find a familiar silhouette, and my gaze rose to find an annoyed set of eyes trained on the hand gripping my arm. It looked like he was waiting for the go ahead to tear it off.

A gasp escaped my lips as I looked at my very pissed off ex-boyfriend. "*Andrew?*"

The rising tension was almost palpable in the small area we occupied. Andrew was there, standing next to me, ready to rip Nathan apart. A pissing contest seemed to commence while Nathan's hand remained in place, his fingers still digging into my arm.

"Let go of the lady," Andrew warned, fists clenching at his side.

Nathan's eyes flickered to mine before going back to Andrew. Instead of releasing me, he pulled me closer to him. Andrew's hand reached out to grab Nathan, and I knew what I had to do.

Stepping between the two, I grabbed the front of their shirts and pushed them apart with as much force as I could muster. Which, considering their sizes compared to my own, wasn't much.

"Enough! Jesus, knock it off." I glared at them. "Nathan, you can let go now. Drew, back off."

"He was grabbing your arm, Lila. *Hard*." Drew's steely gaze was leveled on Nathan.

"Yes, after saving me from some drunk sleaze on the dance floor," I explained. Well, it was pretty much true. "Then he proceeded to lecture my drunk ass about watching out for myself."

Andrew's jaw opened and then closed, looking from me to Nathan. "Really?" He looked like he was still dubious of Nathan's reaction and harsh grip, which was warranted as Nathan was still on the defensive side.

"What's going on?" Caroline came up to us, her eyes taking in our stance.

"Just a misunderstanding and too much testosterone," I assured her.

Andrew visibly relaxed, but continued to be on his guard. It took Nathan longer. What had Nathan been about to say? My stomach churned as an insane curiosity swept through me. And what was he so angry about now?

"Okay, then," Caroline said, looking between all of us. "We ordered another round of drinks back at the table. Join us, Drew?"

Andrew's gaze moved down to me as if he was searching for something before answering. "Sounds great, Carrie." His familiar good natured grin lit up his features. He swept me up in his arms for a hug then extended his hand outward, indicating for me to go first. "After you, Lila." It was apparent he didn't trust Nathan enough to let me walk in front of him.

My steps wobbled a bit, the alcohol getting to me more. Nathan's hand reached out to mine, steadying me. I looked up to find his emotions secured back in place, his anger stifled for the moment, hidden away, stewing beneath. His fake smile was plastered in place, and inside I cried out for the real Nathan to show himself again. I wanted to know him, not the pretty picture he presented to the world. Brief glimpses were not enough to satisfy me.

God, we were the perfect pair with the way we handled ourselves.

It would be nice to be normal, not to have to keep the act up all of the time. To end the masquerade.

Somehow the nightmare escalated as I ended up sandwiched between Andrew and Nathan. The most awkward place in the world to be—at least for me. Trapped between the guy I used to date, and the guy who was secretly fucking me into oblivion. It didn't help that Nathan's hand had returned to my thigh under the table.

Andrew hiked his thumb toward Nathan. Subtlety be damned. "Okay, so who's this newbie?"

We all laughed then everyone launched into the whole Vivian debacle that led to Nathan being my new partner in crime. Oh, if they only knew how true that was in reality.

The waitress came by with the round Caroline ordered. I got one sip in before a hand grabbed it from me.

"You don't need that," Andrew said.

My glare was icy as I grabbed the glass back from him, taking multiple large gulps until the majority of the liquid was gone. "Don't mess with my drink, Drew. I need it."

"No, you don't."

"It's the only way I can sleep, okay?" I admitted in a huff, and rubbed my eyes. I was so tired, exhausted to the point of tears. Add in the downers of the booze and I was about to burst. "I just want to get some fucking sleep. I can't fucking drink every night, so let me sleep tonight. I can get more than a couple hours in and my brain will shut down."

Caroline thankfully jumped in, which was good because I didn't want to go into it any further. "Her insomnia's back."

Nathan was already staring at me, I could feel it. My attention moved down to where his hand was, the skin tingling beneath.

"All right, off topic Lila. I'm not interesting enough. Next topic," I rambled, trying to steer the conversation away from my depressing self.

Andrew snorted. "I see you still love to be the center of attention."

I rolled my eyes, which caused my whole head to spin. "Yeah, yeah. Drunk, depressed, center-of-attention-hating, stupid, ugly…" I choked as the words began swirling in my head. I tilted the rest of my drink back, trying to drown them out.

"Okay, enough." Andrew took the glass out of my shaking hand. "I think it's time to get your drunken ass home."

I let out a whimpering sigh. "I drove."

"You definitely aren't driving. I can take you," Andrew said.

Nathan's fingers dug into my thigh, and I could swear I heard him growl. "I can take her home."

Everyone at the table turned to stare at him, myself included. I couldn't hold back the laughter that escaped. "Oh, Caroline, I forgot to tell you." I placed my hand near my mouth to block people from hearing as I whispered across to her. "The asshole lives in my building!"

"You know I can hear you, right, drunkie?" Nathan quirked his brow at me, while his fingers caressed my thigh. It was a dangerous thing to do in the company we were keeping, but I loved it.

I turned to him, contemplating what to say in response. He was distracting me again, not that it was a hard thing for him to do. "Do I look like I care?"

"Don't hold back on me now, Palmer, let it out."

Fine, he wanted to play, my drunk ass would play. "I was going to go into great detail of where to stick it, but thought it might be a little too rough for our party here."

Ian laughed. "Oooh, Lila's getting surly."

"Surly wench, that's my name," I agreed.

Nathan smirked at me. "I'm going to call you that from now on."

I narrowed my eyes at him. "Bite me, Thorne."

"You are so fucking asking for it," he whispered in my ear, his hand sliding up under my skirt.

"Alrighty!" I jumped, startling everyone at the table. "I need…home. Who's taking me?"

Andrew turned to me. "I can, babe."

There went Nathan, glaring at him again. "I live in the same building. Why waste the gas when we're going to the same place?"

And pissing contest round two, commence!

I had to try to pull their attention away from each other. "Asshole has a good point."

"Would you stop calling me that?" Nathan's face turned red and a vein pulsed at his temple. His jaw flexed as he exhaled in a rush.

"Nope. You threatened to call me 'surly wench' at work; if that's the case, I have every right to call you 'asshole.'"

"Are you sure you're okay to go home with him?" Andrew asked; his eyes locked on mine.

"What the hell is that supposed to mean?" The tone of Nathan's voice made the hairs on the back of my neck stand up.

"I just thought you'd want to stick around and pick up someone for dessert," Andrew answered with a smile on his face. It was becoming obvious they didn't care much for one another.

Nathan sneered at Andrew. "No thanks, I'm full."

"And on that note," Caroline piped in.

"On that note, I'm calling it a night and taking 'drunkie' here with me." Nathan scooted out of the booth so I could get out.

"Well, it's been fun all!" I added. "Drew…good to see you."

I had turned to leave when Andrew's arms wrapped around me. "You call me if you need anything, okay? I'll always be here for you, you know that, right?"

"I know, Drew." I placed a chaste kiss on his cheek. "See you."

Nathan led me through the club, his hand wrapped around my wrist as we worked our way to the entrance. It was a silent walk to his car as most of my concentration and energy was focused on walking straight. He held open the door to the car like a gentleman, and I slid in.

The tension was thick in the car, and I didn't have to look at him to know he was riled up. I just hoped he didn't explode before we made it home.

# CHAPTER 8

W e pulled up to our building, and I stumbled out of the car. My body lit up at his closeness, then I felt his hands on me, hoisting me up in the air and over his shoulder.

"Nathan, put me down, damn it. I can walk," I whined as he moved us into the building.

I pounded on his back with my fists as he greeted the night guard, but my attention was diverted by the fine ass in front of me. I could not, and did not want to contain the urge to grab it, so I did. He yelped in surprise as he stepped onto the elevator. I smacked it and his grip on me tightened.

I could feel the growl in his chest, there was no doubt about it. Wetness began to pool from the sound and the anticipation of what he might do to me this time.

We arrived at the fourteenth floor, and he stepped out, walking a few steps; the keys rattled as he unlocked the door. As soon as we entered his condo, Nathan dropped me down onto my feet and had me pinned against the wall with his body, his lips hard on mine. It was a punishing kiss. I didn't know what for, but he was angry about something.

He released my lips. "Who is he, this *Andrew*?"

I blinked at him. Was he jealous? I wanted him to be jealous; it would mean I amounted to something to him.

"Andrew is my ex-boyfriend." I was still confused as I answered. His eyes were hard, his muscles tight. "*Nathan?*"

His lips crashed to mine again before moving away. The sound of splintering drywall filled the room as my eyes opened to find where he had gone.

Nathan's fist was imbedded in the wall.

"Nathan!" I ran to help him pull his hand out. That was when I got a look at the entry wall. Seven. I counted seven other holes in the drywall. "Why?"

I gazed at him, the inexplicable man in front of me. He confused me so much I never knew which way was up.

"You. You do this to me. Every time... You make me so angry," he admitted.

I might have been scared if it hadn't been for the burning in his eyes and his fingertips, caressing my cheek. "I slept with my dress shirt on the other night because it smelled like you, and that pisses me off! I'm mad at myself and pissed at you for wrapping me around your little fucking finger."

"But I didn't..."

"I know!" he yelled, his anger seeping from him. "And that ticks me off more. I hate that you turn me on. I hate the way I

77

need you all the fucking time. I don't want that. I *can't* want that. I *can't* want you…but I do, so fucking much I do."

"I want you, too."

Pain flitted across his face. "I hated every male that even looked at you tonight and wanted to hurt the one that dared touch you. I wanted to scream out *mine* to keep them all at bay. But I can't; I can't claim you like that. I *will* consume you."

"Why me?" The question snuck past my lips before I could stop it. My strength gave out, and I sunk to the floor.

"What did you say?" He seemed to be in complete disbelief as he stared down at me.

"I'm nothing. Drew leaving me proved *them* right. I'm nothing special. Plain, boring, pitiful, ugly Lila. Worthless."

"You shut that shit up right now!" He took a few calming breaths before sitting down on the floor in front of me. "*You* are beautiful, intelligent, witty, sarcastic, fun as hell to tease, and so fucking sexy I have trouble keeping my hands off you. You make it so hard to stay away… I want you so much. I've tried so hard, but you keep fucking drawing me in."

"Then why? Why can't we…"

"Because I can't. I can't love you. I can't allow myself to pursue you, Lila. A beautiful woman like you shouldn't waste your time on me."

"But, you said I wasn't 'that pretty'."

He jumped to his feet startling me. "Shit. I was being a sarcastic asshole and was going to tell you I was joking, but you fucking threw me with your response. I'm used to women arguing against me, but you agreed. That shit is fucked up." He paced in front of me, his brow twisted, fingers tugging at his hair in agitation.

78

I stared at him in disbelief. Boy, drunk me was envisioning quite a different Nathan. He couldn't have admitted all of that. I was delusional. I had to be. Right?

I picked myself up off the floor. "Don't you want to know what I think?"

"No, it doesn't matter."

"It doesn't matter that I want you?"

His jaw tightened, and his eyes squeezed shut. "Please don't."

I looked up at him, my head tilting, trying to find the words for the idea rattling in my head. It wasn't much, but it would be something. I was pathetic enough to settle for something.

"We can't...be?"

"*Be*? Be, how?"

"Like we have been?"

He pushed the palms of his hands into his eyes. "You don't really want that with me."

"What if I do?"

"Drop it, Lila." His tone was harsh and silenced me. I had gotten more out of him tonight than I ever expected to.

"Well, goodnight then." I turned toward the door. His hand caught my wrist and spun me around.

"Where the fuck do you think you're going?"

"Home." I wasn't home, I was at his place, and I just wanted to get out of it.

"Oh, no. I'm not letting you out of my sight, drunkie." He pulled me away from the door, making sure I couldn't leave. My eyes roamed around while we moved through his condo and I was astonished. It looked nothing like what I thought it would. I expected lavish furniture and decorations due to the price tag on his place, but there was little of either. The walls were bare, and the furniture was sparse.

We entered the bedroom and he sat me on the bed before kneeling in front of me and proceeding to take off my boots.

My fingers brushed through his hair. "So silky," I murmured.

He leaned into my touch for a brief moment, then swiftly moved out of my reach. He grabbed my waist and lifted me to where I was bending over his shoulder. His fingers found the zipper to my skirt and slid it off me, tossing it somewhere on the floor of the dark room.

"You do know I'm not so drunk that I can't walk or undress myself, right?"

"Shut up and get in the bed, Delilah," he commanded.

Was it wrong that I loved when he directed me like that?

I obliged and snuggled under the covers. They smelled of him, and I found a new happy place, wrapped around the musky and spicy scent that was Nathan. I was sure my therapist would like that. He never felt my happy place was happy enough.

I woke a few hours later wrapped up in Nathan's arms. It was warm and inviting and I wanted it. I wanted him. Could I do it? Could I show him it was okay to love? Maybe it was best to go with the flow. Maybe we could both heal. What would Dr. Morgenson say? Shit, I needed to see him again; it'd been too long, several months.

I turned my head to look at him, taking in how peaceful his face was when he was asleep. I sighed as I moved to sit up; I needed to go home. It was too intoxicating being so close to him. I was drowning in Nathan.

"No," he mumbled. "Stay."

His arms pulled me back into his body, lips kissing my shoulder, nipping the skin beneath as his fingers flexed around my waist. His tongue slid out, tasting my skin, his hand moving down my stomach and teasing the skin at the top of my panties. He slid beneath the fabric and two of his fingers found my opening, pushing deep inside.

I cried out at the intrusion, one I'd been aching for. "Fuck!"

His hips rocked against my ass, his hard length pressing into me. "Mmm, your pussy gets so fucking wet for me. Do you get this wet for other cocks, or just mine? Hmm?"

My body arched under his assault. His other hand moved to pinch my nipples. I couldn't stop the rocking of my hips, pushing farther down on his hand. I needed him deeper. "Nate… mmm, only you."

"Good girl," he said. "Or should I say naughty? Only naughty girls get this fucking soaked. Listen to you moaning like a whore. You love my fingers buried inside you, don't you? Not as much as you love my cock filling you to the hilt though." His whispers were gruff and needy.

"Fuck no. You...oh God…filling me with your…fuck..." I moaned, barely able to keep myself from screaming incoherent sounds at his onslaught of my pussy. "Cock! Please!"

His body left mine, his hand turning me onto my back as he slipped between my thighs. His clothed cock nestled against my wet center, while his lips found mine for a searing kiss.

"This what you want? Right here?" He accentuated his words with a thrust of his hips, hitting my clit just right, making me scream out.

"Yes, yes, please." I really was a slut for him, but only for him. He pulled my shirt over my head, tossing it on the floor, my bra following.

He leaned down and took my nipple into his mouth, his teeth scraping across my skin, fingers digging into my hips before hooking into my panties and pulling them down my legs. I pulled his shirt up and over his head while he pushed his pants down, freeing his straining cock. I licked my lips, wanting to taste, but was pushed back down on my back.

I could feel him at my opening a split second before he slid in, cursing as his forehead rested on mine.

"So fucking tight...every time. Why do you have to be so goddamn fucking tight?"

He rocked his hips until he was all the way in, and I felt full, whole. His arms wrapped around me, pulling our bodies flush as his hips began to move. There was a tenderness replacing the usual frenzy, a shift from what was and entering the possibility of what could be.

His hands, which were usually rough, were sensual, his need focused. His kisses were still hard, just calmer. It was like he was trying to burn himself into me with each slow, steady touch. I was caged in his arms. He was keeping me as close as possible; his head in the crook of my neck. His hips were slower, driving his cock into me in long strokes.

"Baby, you feel so fucking good," he whispered into my ear. "So sexy, so fucking irresistible. Don't want to fight it anymore. Beautiful Lila. You make me crazy."

It was a slow burn, my body humming with each thrust in and whimpering with each stroke out, our bodies rocking together. It was unlike anything I had ever experienced. The fire consumed me, my body and my heart opening up to him.

"You like that, don't you? Oh, shit...you...you like my cock thrusting into you, don't you?" he asked, wanting an answer.

"That's how dirty of a slut you are. Tell me—you like my cock always pumping into you?"

"No."

"No?" he questioned, his voice losing the confident edge it held. He sounded unsure, his hips stopped moving, leaving him buried to the hilt. I had a hard time concentrating on anything at all when he was that deep inside me.

"No. I love it."

"Fuck, shit." His hips dug harder as his grip tightened. Speed increased, his teeth biting into my shoulder. I was getting close, whimpering at every movement.

If possible, he held me closer. His groans of pleasure had me shaking, sitting on the edge of my orgasm. I was panting into his neck, just behind his ear.

I wanted to mark him as he marked me, and I found my spot. I licked at his skin, tasting the saltiness of it. My mouth clamped onto the tendon right below his ear, sucking hard before my teeth pushed into his skin. Hard enough to mark, but not hard enough to break skin. Like he did to me.

"Shit!" he cried out, his thrusts becoming erratic.

I tipped over the edge, and screamed out his name as my pussy clenched around him. "Nate!"

"That's it, baby, fucking come. Shit, shit. Oh, fuck. You really do love this shit." His body started shaking as his hips stilled. Our eyes were locked with one another, his hooded and glazed, and I was certain mine matched. I felt him emptying inside me, and I shuddered in ecstasy.

After his orgasm, his arms gave out, no longer able to hold his weight. He fell to the side, landing next to me on the bed, and pulled me up so that my head was resting on his chest.

Hours later, I awoke with the need to use the bathroom, prying myself from the death grip he had on me. Once done, I walked back into the bedroom and gazed at his sleeping form.

The light was starting to come in through the windows, illuminating his body. He was lying there, naked, the sheet barely covering below the waist, one of his legs sticking out. I had never seen him naked before; he had always been half dressed. But in that moment I could admire him in all his glory.

I walked closer to the bed and my stomach dropped. The sight before me was horrific. I felt as though I'd been punched in the gut.

A thick, jagged and raised pink scar ran on his left side from his ribs, down his side, and around his hip. It wasn't the only scar. Some were jagged, others straight, but all were smaller than the one on his side, marring his beautiful body. There were holes next to some, indicating the wound had been stitched or stapled up. His left leg held the second largest scar, and it ran from above his knee to halfway down his shin. I studied his face as I tried to keep myself together. That was when I noticed the star shaped scar in his hairline, right above his ear.

It was part of his puzzle, a big piece of his mystery. Something had happened to him, something terrible, and he shut himself off to everything. My heart was breaking as I took in the sight of the evidence of his once broken body.

Tears flowed in steady streams down my face when I dropped to the ground, my legs giving out. I erupted in violent shakes, arms wrapping around my body, trying desperately to keep the sob that was threatening to escape within me.

"Lila?" His voice was groggy and thick with sleep. He jumped out of bed and stood in front of me, giving me the full view of his body and all the damage that had been inflicted. The sob broke from my chest, and it was painful and raw. "*Lila?*"

He dropped down on the ground in front of me, and I flung my arms around his neck, pulling him close. Tears were falling from my eyes as his arms wrapped around my body, his head dipping into the crook of my neck.

"What happened? What happened to you?" I asked through my sobs. His grip grew tighter as if he was using my body to hold his own together, to keep himself from breaking.

"Please, don't ask me that. Please… I can't…"

We held each other on the floor for what seemed like hours until my tears stopped. I leaned away from him to see a frightened look in his eyes. My gaze wandered his body, my fingers reaching out to trace the large scar around his hip. He didn't flinch at my investigation, but stared at me in wonder.

He leaned in and took my bottom lip between his teeth, staring into my eyes. He was searching for something, but he couldn't find it.

"Push me away; you have to," he demanded. His eyes were haunted and scared.

"No."

"*Push me away!*"

"*I can't!*" I cried out, the tears returning.

His body sagged. "Why? Tell me why…say it."

My heart was breaking for the hollow, empty shell of a man in front of me. "Because I want you! I want you so much it hurts! I need all of you, and I can't deny it anymore."

He looked down at me, his inner conflict and turmoil evident on his face.

His fingers brushed strands of hair behind my ear as he cupped my face. "I can't give you what you want, beautiful. I'll only hurt you."

"It's okay. If it's you, I don't mind."

"Stop," he pleaded, his hands coming up in surrender. "Let's just go back to bed."

"Okay…okay."

With that, we returned to the sanctuary that was his bed, and curled up in each other's arms. It seemed to be what we both wanted, what we both needed. He was relenting, if even a little, and letting himself simply be.

# CHAPTER 9

I t'd been a week since I admitted to myself I was altered. That *Nathan* had altered me. The growing feelings for him I'd kept hidden, were out. The night after we left the club made me face that fact. How I thought and felt about him changed; he wasn't the asshole I thought he was when I first met him. He was a broken man, and it made me wonder – can two broken souls make one whole person?

He intrigued me, it wasn't only sex anymore. Every time his guard dropped around me, I saw the real Nathan, and I liked him. I wanted him. Every day I needed him more. Any thought of leaving him and returning to the way we were, was painful.

One week had passed since he conceded to letting himself have *something* with me. It was undefined and not spoken about out loud; little different than it was in the beginning. The exception was every night he was either in my bed or I was in his. It started on Saturday night when he showed up at my door just before midnight and took me against the wall in the entryway.

For three nights in a row, I was running to answer his knock near midnight. He'd fucked me like I'd never been fucked before. His eyes were dark and angry as he snarled at me; always reminding me he believed his lust for me was my fault. Hands dug into my flesh, bruising me. They were harsh as he pulled me to him, at the same time he pushed me away. Then we'd crawl into bed and fall sleep, his arms wrapped around me with the same intensity he'd used to fuck me.

On the fourth night, things changed. It was past midnight and he hadn't knocked on my door. I knew of his struggle, and if I truly wanted him, I was going to have to fight for him. So, a few minutes before one in the morning, I knocked on *his* door and fucked *him* into oblivion then collapsed, exhausted, in *his* bed.

I'd never had such a peaceful sleep. The cure for my insomnia appeared to be a hard fucking, as I had passed out every night and did not wake until the alarm went off the next morning.

That lasted until the wee hours of Saturday morning when I felt the bed shake before Nathan screamed out—a sound so raw and harrowing, I knew it would haunt me for the rest of my life.

His body was shaking, his chest gasping for air as he swung his legs around the side of the bed. He fumbled in the dark with the light switch, and I cringed against the sudden, intense glow that filled the room. I couldn't see anything, but I heard a drawer open, and the clinking of plastic and what sounded like pills bouncing around. Frustrated sounds and movements came from him in his frantic search. Once he found the right bottle, he opened a container and threw his head back.

I crawled out from under the comforter to sit next to him, my eyes having adjusted to the light. He must have felt the bed move, because his hand shot out and pushed the drawer closed, as if he didn't want me to see the contents inside. He was still breathing hard, his face contorted in pain and anguish. My chest constricted; his agony became mine. It was so overpowering at times; I wondered how he even managed day-to-day tasks. Or was it my presence? It was always me that set him off, that much I knew. He never did explain why, other than he was angry at himself for wanting me and giving into that want to some degree.

My hands reached up to cup his face. His pained gaze met mine as he leaned into my touch.

"Ssshhh," I soothed, my other hand stroking the sweat matted hair from his face. "It's all right, baby. Everything's all right."

His lips caught mine in a harsh kiss. He didn't say anything, but pulled me close as we lay back down. His arms wrapped around my body, head lowering to the crook of my neck. My hands began running through his hair.

After a while he calmed and I could feel the even temper of his breath blowing across my chest. Tears stung my eyes, but I pushed them back. I needed to be stronger if I was going to help him; a large feat for me.

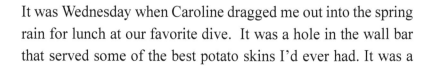

It was Wednesday when Caroline dragged me out into the spring rain for lunch at our favorite dive. It was a hole in the wall bar that served some of the best potato skins I'd ever had. It was a rare treat to split an order, and I was willing to brave the weather for the wonderful tastes that awaited.

We placed our order and included side salads to make it a little less terrible.

"So, you got laid?" she asked without missing a beat.

I choked on the drink as it went down the wrong pipe, and almost spit some of my soda across the table at her. "W-what?"

"You heard me. You. Got. Laid."

"How... Why do you think that?"

"Oh, come on, Lila. I've known you since we interned together between L2 and L3. That's five years, if you're trying to figure it out."

I sighed. "Fine. Yes, I got laid. Happy?"

"No. Who is he?" She was not letting the subject go, her lips curling into a smile.

"Just some guy I met," I lied, trying to brush it off. I wanted to tell her it was Nathan, but how was I supposed to explain our situation? I didn't want to tell her about his scars and his self-imposed inability to love. I didn't want to gossip about his pain. I wanted to protect him. I needed Nathan. So, I would lie to my best friend for now in the hopes that soon I could tell her everything.

"And?" she pressed. "Name? Date of birth? Social security number? Birthmarks and tattoos?" She grinned and waggled her eyebrows.

I laughed at her absurdity, and it felt good. "His name?" I felt the blood leech out of my face. My mind raced to come up with something when Nathan's middle name popped up. I remembered seeing it on some of his access paperwork. "Christopher, his name is Christopher."

"Was he at the club the other night?"

Oh, thank the heavens, something I didn't have to lie about. "Yeah."

"Well, obviously you liked him enough to have fun with him on multiple occasions."

I couldn't help the sad smile that formed on my face. "I like him, I do."

"*But?*"

"But, he has some issues he's working through, so I'm not really sure how he feels about me."

"Well, if you can keep your self-flogging at bay, maybe you two can help each other. It's obvious he likes something about you if he keeps coming back for more."

"The feeling of me wrapped around his..." I trailed off, the waiter smirking as he dropped our food off.

Caroline laughed, and I couldn't help but join in. I felt lighter after telling her, even though it wasn't much. It felt good to talk about him in some fashion to someone other than myself. We ate our treats and headed back to the office, and I went straight back to the mysterious God that sat in the desk next to me.

---

Two days later, I was squirming in my chair, my mind envisioning the previous evening's activities, and it was making my panties soaked. Every day seemed to be growing longer; minutes where like hours. His scent filled the confines of our office, making my cravings for him stronger with each tick of the clock. I wanted him all the damn time.

I absently twirled a pen in my mouth as I attempted to read over the contract in front of me. It had been a day for reading and re-reading, and starting over because I didn't catch anything. I didn't even realize I had begun daydreaming, the pen sliding between my lips, until my phone began to buzz, breaking me from my trance. It was a text from Nathan, sitting right next to me. I'd forgotten we exchanged numbers. Curious, I opened the message and wished I hadn't. It was too much for me to handle.

*If you keep sucking on that pen I WILL drag you off to a secluded spot and shove my cock in your mouth.*

My eyes widened and I choked on said pen while I read his text. The message was so hot my whole body lit up, and I licked my lips at the thought. Fantasies began running rampant, about places he would drag me to, when my phone buzzed with another message from him.

*And you will choke like that around my cock when I jam it all the way down your fucking tease of a throat.*

I had to begin fanning myself with the still unread contract; I was certain my face was Santa-suit red.

"Hey, Delilah," Benjamin called from the doorway. "Can I get your help on this verbiage...? You okay?"

I gave him a fake smile. "Fine, just got a little hot all of the sudden."

"Well, keep your cooties to yourself. Marianne will kill me if I bring home another illness from work," he said with a laugh. Benjamin was such a sweet guy, and his very pregnant wife had gotten sick earlier in the year and she was unable to take much medicine, adding to her increasing level of discomfort.

"I'm not sure that what's wrong with Delilah is contagious," Nathan spoke, interrupting our conversation, his eyes trained on the screen in front of him.

I quirked my brow at him. "And exactly what is 'wrong' with me?"

"Few screws loose there, drunkie. Now, be a dear and help Benjamin out so you can get back to drooling all over the Henderson contract," he taunted.

"Screw you." I scowled at him and turned back to Benjamin. "So, verbiage?"

I worked with him for about half an hour before returning to my attempt at concentrating on my work. A difficult task when I was still so worked up from the texts Nathan had sent me.

It was after six when we saw Benjamin again, dropping by to let us know everyone was gone, and to lock up when we left. I sat stock still at my desk, paralyzed. A sudden extreme awareness of Nathan, and how we were alone, hit me. The words of his texts came back to me, and a small moan slipped from my lips. Out of the corner of my eye, I could see him look briefly at me before resuming his work.

After a few minutes of pin-drop silence, Nathan rose from his chair and walked to the door. He reached out and slammed it shut, the sound making me jump. My breathing became labored, my body shaking in anticipation as I heard the click of the lock. He turned toward me; his eyes were dark, menacing, and full of lust.

He stared at me as his fingers worked to undo his tie, while he stalked his way over to me.

"You have been a very naughty girl today." His hand wrapped around the fabric, slipping it from around his neck. "Naughty girls get punished. *Hard.* I don't think I can wait any longer to punish you…"

My thighs were rubbing together, my bottom lip caught between my teeth to stifle the moan that threatened to escape. It was too late, the look in his eyes was animalistic, and I was dripping for him. He grabbed my arm, pulling me to my feet, and turned me around. My arms were pinned behind my back, the silk of his tie wrapping around my wrists, binding them.

He plopped me back down in my chair, giving me a fierce kiss before straightening to reach for his zipper. His fingers lowered it, making me fight off the shiver at the sound of the metal teeth clicking. He pulled his cock out of the slit, took a step closer, lining the tip mere inches from my lips. The urge to touch him was great, but I couldn't; I was restrained from doing just that.

"Kiss it," he demanded. I leaned forward as best as I could, limited without the use of my arms. My tongue flicked out and licked the underside of the head. Nathan's fist wrapped around my hair and pulled tight so I was looking up at him. "I told you to kiss it, Delilah."

He released me. I parted my lips, and kissed right at his slit, tasting his salty tang. I placed hot open mouth kisses down his length and back up to his hot, red tip.

"Good girl. Now open wide."

My mouth opened in time for him to impatiently push forward. I gagged as he hit the back of my throat, unprepared for him.

"Mmm, that's it, baby. Shit, your mouth is so fucking good." His hips thrust him in and out. I was only taking him about halfway.

Impatient, he thrust all the way in and I did what he said I'd do: I choked on him.

He chuckled and stared at his cock as it moved between my lips, his eyes morphing into slits. They looked like they were fighting to remain open. His mouth slack, lips parted.

He took a deep breath and seemed to re-center himself. "I told you you'd choke on it. You like that, don't you, baby? You have the best fucking mouth. Love watching my cock disappear between your hot little lips. You're a little cock slut, sucking me in like that. Shit, so fucking good."

His fingers tightened in my hair, his other hand joining as he began to drive his cock down my throat. I moved my tongue along the underside, and suctioned as best I could around him, spurring more sounds of pleasure out of him; obscenities kept stumbling from his lips.

As always, his words had my panties soaked through, and I was certain a wet spot was seeping through my skirt. My eyes watered a little with each harsh thrust of his hips, but I took everything he gave me. Because it was all about him. My punishment for teasing him, and I'd take it again and again with a smile on my face.

My body began to ache, the inability to move my arms, coupled with my leaning forward, was burning muscles I wasn't accustomed to using.

His thrusts became erratic, his cock hardening even more, and I knew he was close.

"Swallow it all. Every fucking last drop," he ordered before pushing forward, pulling my head down to the base as he twitched and emptied down my throat. I gagged around him, tasting him as he poured into my mouth.

My tongue swirled around the length, licking him clean as he pulled out. His breath was coming out in hard gasps, and he leaned back against the edge of my desk for support.

"Holy shit, baby, that was…fuck that was excellent," he said with a lazy smile.

I grinned up at him and leaned forward to kiss the drop that was leaking from the tip. He moaned and twitched, his lips crashing down on mine for a hungry thankful kiss, tasting himself still on my tongue.

He fastened his zipper and then helped me up, a difficult task since my knees were still shaking from want and desire. He freed my wrists, massaging and kissing where the fabric had dug in.

His hand slapped my ass, and I squealed in surprise, then he walked back around to his desk. "Back to work, Palmer.

I stared at him in disbelief. Was he really going to leave me in such a state? I whimpered as he took his seat. "You're mean."

"Well, maybe that will keep you from playing with your pen in your mouth."

I gave him a wicked smile and licked my lips. "Or maybe it gave me the idea to do it more."

He groaned and rubbed his face. "Lila…"

I looked at him with raised eyebrows. "I'm not the one who's so impatient. I can wait an hour."

He rolled his eyes and shook his head. "You just called me mean for not fucking you right here and now."

"That's because I'm all wet, soaking through my panties."

"Serves you right. You've kept me hard all fucking day. Back to work." He twirled his finger as he pointed to my chair.

With a huff, I sat back down and, with a sort of urgency, returned to my work.

# CHAPTER 10

It was almost eight when we rolled into the parking lot of our building. We walked up and greeted the night guard, then stepped onto an awaiting elevator. As we entered, Nathan pressed the buttons for our respective floors, indicating tonight would be the same as the previous nights. Denial overpowering our want until one of us broke sometime during the night.

I should have grabbed him the second the doors closed, but I lacked the courage. Odd how his emotions ebbed and flowed like the tide, constantly changing the dynamics of whatever it was we were to each other. His moods always set our tone. At that moment he was rebelling against us, trying to ignore the pull we both felt. Did he feel guilty for giving in at the office?

The air around us changed the second his stomach let it be known it wanted food, the grumble echoing around the elevator.

A giggle escaped before I turned to grin at him. "Hungry are we?" I watched his body relax, a sheepish grin forming. It was new, and I couldn't help but think how cute he looked.

"Maybe just a little."

The elevator pinged, signaling we had reached my floor. I stepped off and extended my hand to him. "Come."

He stared at me like he was contemplating what I meant. "Lila, I…"

"Have dinner with me. Come."

"You don't have to cook for me," he said.

"Well, I have to do it for me, and it's usually enough to feed four. So, come." I beckoned him with my hand.

After a moment of deliberation and great reluctance, along with an argument from his stomach, he took my hand. He stared at me with his brow knitted together while we walked down the hall to my condo. I didn't know what was going through his mind, but from the outside it looked as if he was guarding himself from my sexual assault. The thought made me laugh as it was he who attacked me in the most spectacular way against a wall in our office. And he was frightened of little me?

"So, how long have you lived in Indianapolis?" I asked while I moved to the bedroom and changed into something more comfortable. We knew few details about one another, and I was going to get to the bottom of Nathan Thorne.

"My whole life, with the exception of college. What about you?" he asked.

He removed his tie and I licked my lips in memory of how he'd used it earlier. He also rid himself of his suit jacket and unbuttoned his dress shirt.

"Indiana native, born and bred," I admitted. "I moved to Indy just before college and stayed. No reason to return anyway. Not much demand for lawyers in the middle of nowhere."

He sounded surprised by my admission. "You didn't go out of state for law school?"

I moved past him and walked to the kitchen.

I sighed and shook my head. "No. Too much to pay out of state tuition. I'll be paying off my school debts for another few years as it is. Even with my grants."

He smirked before admitting his parents had paid for college, including his stint at Harvard Law. I stared at him as he spoke of the East Coast school and his time there. He was smiling as he recounted his first year at the elite establishment.

I had always known he was more than just a transactional attorney. You didn't go to Harvard Law for such a technical position. Another piece.

I admired his smile before commenting, "You know, that mask of yours is slipping a lot lately."

He shrugged his shoulders, his smile faltering. "There's no point in the pretense around you."

My heart fluttered in my chest. "But I still don't know your secrets," I pointed out as I opened the fridge door, and dipped down to find some vegetables for a salad.

"No, but you know there *are* secrets. That's much more than anyone else. It's nice not to have to always pretend everything's perfect."

I, better than anyone, knew what he meant. Even his voice had lost its pretense and was low with little inflection.

"So, why pretend then?"

"It makes things easier." He rubbed the back of his neck. It seemed a nervous gesture to me; he didn't like the subject matter. "It didn't take long to learn that after… People don't really want to know that your knee and wrist ache every day, your body hurts in ways you can't describe, that you're plagued by migraines and nightmares, or your depression and anxiety continue years later."

I stood staring at him after his impromptu confession. He hadn't given much detail, but at least I knew why. It was easier than the truth by far. It kept looks of pity at bay. It kept the memories away.

"What about you?" he asked.

I pulled away from the open door, bringing with me a variety of vegetables and a can of pasta sauce. Pasta was quick, which was good due to how late it was, according to the wall clock.

"What *about* me?"

He quirked an eyebrow at me. "You really want to play that game? Do you want me to say it?"

"No."

"Why then?"

"The same. It's easier to say I'm fine then go into detail about how I put out a confident front, but inside I'm holding the darkness at bay and one word can send it crashing down."

"You confound me," he said.

My brow scrunched as I stared back at him in confusion.

"You have such a poor view of yourself." He frowned, deep in thought, and his voice was full of concern. "How did you get this way?"

"Doesn't matter. Damage done, and I'm working to get past it." I swallowed hard, turning away from him as I located a cutting board and knife.

He settled his hip into the side of the counter, keeping out of my way as I worked. His position meant he could continue to talk to me and also watch my every move. "Hiding it doesn't help you get past it."

"No, it doesn't, you know that all too well. The thing is: I've at least gotten a little better over the years. Have you?" I asked as I filled a pot with water and set it on the burner, turning it on high to get it boiling.

"Your eyes say differently," he said, diverting away from my question yet again.

"I said I've gotten better, not that I was healed. Downers don't help, that's why I don't go out drinking with people... you've seen what happens."

"Yes, but that also shows you aren't better."

"You make me better," I whispered in a small voice.

He blinked at me, his face stoic.

"You make me feel like I'm all of the things they said I wasn't. Beautiful, smart, sexy...worth something."

"Who are 'they'?" Nathan asked after a moment of silence. "What did 'they' do to you?"

"You want to know? You're certain you want me to tell you how every day I was told how insignificant I was?" I set down the knife and turned toward him, my arms crossing over my chest. "You're not forthcoming with information, and I get that, I do. I hope one day you'll be able to tell me. As for me... Well, when you're young, and the people in your life tell you these things *every day,* you begin to believe them. They become ingrained into who you are, and I've worked damn hard to push them away. Years of therapy. I've seen a psychiatrist from the time I was seventeen. Twelve years later I have more confidence, but everything still haunts me."

"I've done that to you, haven't I? I've said something to trigger you?" His tone was knowing.

"You didn't know," I said with a shrug, looking away. "Alcohol is a double edged sword for me. It helps me sleep, but my depression spikes."

"Yet you drink every Friday, letting everything come back," he noted.

"Stalking me now?" I teased.

"No, just observant."

"Well, Mr. Observant, can you hand me the bread sitting next to you?"

I placed the vegetables on a cutting board and rinsed my hands. My skin prickled with the familiar humming that passed between us, letting me know he was in very close proximity. I took the bread from him, letting out a breath. The back of his fingers caressed my cheeks as his gaze captured mine.

"You are so much more than pretty. That was what I wanted to say to you that night. Instead I was inadvertently mean to push you away." He pressed his body against me, pushing me into the counter. His forehead fell forward, resting against my own. "How do you do this to me?"

With a small tentative move, I tilted my head, testing him, giving him an out before my lips found his. He didn't move at first, didn't breathe, but then his hands were in my hair, his tongue slipping in to find mine, his teeth biting my bottom lip when he gave in.

"Fuck, you taste so good. Could fucking eat *you* for dinner," he said with a growl, his hips rocking forward, pressing his cock into my stomach. He was hard and my eyes closed from the euphoric feeling of what I wanted.

"Please."

"Please what?" he asked. His hand moved down to my ass, squeezing it, pulling me closer to him as he continued to rock into me.

My fingers clenched around the fabric of his shirt, the heat in my cheeks rising. "Please, Nathan, I need you to fuck me. I need you inside me. I've waited all day."

I received a moan of appreciation as the hand in my hair tilted my head back and his mouth began its journey down my neck. I was panting with need, still so worked up from earlier.

He was unable to take any more, and lifted me up onto the counter. My legs wrapped around his waist, and the new position had him lined up with my throbbing pussy. He pushed his hips into mine, rubbing the length of his clothed cock against me. I moaned at the sensation, what I'd been dreaming about all day.

"You like that? Little wanton slut begging for my cock. Is that what you want? Me to shove my cock in you? Make you scream?"

"Yes, fuck yes!" I pulled him back down to my lips. We shifted again as need took over.

We worked to remove our clothing as swiftly as possible. It was difficult, what with our lips crashing together, and hands doing anything we could to get closer, but somehow we managed to remove them.

"Fuck." He shuddered as I took his cock in my hand, stroking him. "God, you are so fucking insatiable."

"Good thing you can keep up," I managed to say as he lined up and pushed his hips forward, filling me one inch at a time.

"So wet for me," he moaned as he pulled out and slid back in, his hips stilling.

His mouth moved down to my nipple, teasing it, the sensation sky rocketing down to my abdomen. I mewled, my hips trying to get him to move. My scalp cried out as he pulled my head back, exposing my neck, bowing my body and granting him access.

His gaze was commanding as he sneered at me. "I'll fuck you when I'm good and ready. Until then you will sit there with my cock shoved up your cunt and be happy it's there."

A shiver ran down my spine at his words, and I complied. His hand moved down to where we were joined and his fingers began teasing my clit. I whimpered as the fire grew, my walls clenching around him, every flick of his fingers or tongue making me tighter. After a few minutes, his need to move took over. He started with short strokes that drove me insane. His teeth pulled on my nipple, and it was the final straw. My orgasm ripped through me, leaving me shaking.

"That's it, baby, come all over my cock."

Nathan released my hair, his hips beginning the punishing pace my body had become accustomed to. He'd given me no time to recover, and I was crying out, screaming; my body still so sensitive. I had no words, just sounds. My vision was blurred, unable to focus, my mind blank. Only my body remained to receive him and the pleasure he gave me.

He was shouting expletives, but I couldn't understand anything other than his large cock slamming into me, his hands gripping me tight, and his mouth marking me. He forced my body over the edge again, and I felt tears running down my cheeks. I was literally crying from the onslaught of sensations.

"Shit, shit, shit!" His hips stilled; he was grunting and groaning as he came deep inside, sheathed to the hilt.

His body relaxed against the cabinets as he came down from the high. Our chests were heaving as our pants died down. My limp arms wrapped around his neck keeping him close. "Lila... fuck, Lila."

"No. No fuck Lila. Lila done for tonight. Try back in the morning," I managed to say. I received a chuckle to my neck in response, and a light kiss against my skin.

"I suppose I could wait a few more hours, maybe fuck you while you're asleep in the middle of the night. Wouldn't that be a nice way to wake up? My cock buried inside of you?"

I moaned at the thought. "Oh, God!"

"I'll take that as a hell yes, Miss Palmer."

"I am all for wake up calls like that, Mr. Thorne."

Steam filling the room drew my attention away from him—the pot was at a rapid boil. Nathan stepped back, and I shuddered as he slipped out of me. He helped me down from the counter before locating a towel to clean us up. My feet touched the cold tile floor, and I turned to shut off the boiling water, but my legs failed me and I stumbled back into him.

He chuckled, his arms wrapping around me as he kissed my neck. "Hmm, maybe we should have something delivered instead of putting you near a pot of boiling water right now."

"You may be on to something." My legs gave out, and I sank to the floor, laughing the whole time.

Two hours later, we were full of fried rice and cashew chicken, lying in my bed. My head rested on his chest, and his fingers were lightly running through my hair.

"Hey, Nathan?" My eyes and body were heavy, sleep closing in.

"Hmm?"

"I'm yours, just so you know," I mumbled, my mind drifting off into the dark of sleep before he could respond.

# CHAPTER 11

Nathan never brought up my declaration in the following weeks. At least not in words. Sometimes I caught his expression flicker, like he was thinking about what I told him—about being his. It faded as soon as it showed up, and I figured that the thought of it made him edgy.

Every day his agitation grew. It was subtle, hiding in his perfected act, so most people didn't notice, but I knew him better than they did. His fingers combed and tugged at his hair and neck more often, his leg bounced in an increasing tempo, and his fuse became shorter.

All-in-all, he was a ticking time bomb.

His nightmares shook the bed almost every night. His grip was bone crushing as he clung to me, trying to keep it all in. I soothed him as best I could, but I knew it would take more than me to fix him. He needed to let it all out, not keep it in. Purge himself of the emotions he kept tightly locked away. Pot calling the kettle, coming from me, but his pain was earth shattering compared to my own.

Over time, I learned he was taking a myriad of drugs daily. Anti-anxiety, anti-depressant, pain medications; I didn't know everything he was ingesting, but I had a feeling some of them he was taking more than he did before and it was because of me. The effect I had on him, and the demons I caused to surface, were too much. He could try to deny it, but there was no point in hiding from me. Not *me*.

I was amazed at how well I was beginning to read Nathan when we were in the office. His discomfort for the Boob-Squad was clear, but no one else could tell.

I sat in my chair, pretending to work, when in reality I was gauging his reaction, trying to figure out why he didn't tell the Boob-Squad to leave him alone once and for all.

His muscles tensed with every passing minute, and he was *not* good.

Tiffany, member number three, was clamoring for his attentions. Leaning toward him, the top two buttons of her blouse were undone, exposing the top of her breasts as she reached to point at some arbitrary word on a summons her client had received.

In my peripheral, I watched him try to avoid looking down her shirt, not wanting to give her any opening, eluding to his disinterest. However, he was a man with breasts being flashed at him, it wasn't like he could resist their call for long. Even from my angle I could see right down her shirt and her ample assets were straining against the hot pink lace of her bra. Of course he was staring at her tits. It was like a fucking neon sign drawing people in. Who could resist that? Even I was having a difficult time looking away.

One small glance spurred her on, and she walked around to his side of the desk so she didn't have to read it upside down. To most it looked like he was making room for her, moving over and back a bit. To me, I saw him fleeing, trying to keep space between them.

I was pretty sure if I hadn't been there, she would have taken it as an invitation to mount him.

Despite his disinterest in the women in the office, especially the Boob-Squad, I knew he was attracted to many of his female colleagues.

I caught him sneaking a peek when he thought no one was looking. It didn't bother me. We weren't in a relationship, at least in the technical sense, and I knew he was only looking; he had no interest in acting on the attraction.

I learned a lot about him by observation; I was a people watcher. His cocky attitude wasn't exactly a lie or an act. It was all based on the man he used to be; a smooth, charismatic, arrogant, intelligent, and fuck hot God. He was playing himself in a role that was no longer his life.

I broke down and asked him one night at dinner about Ian's comment of him being a playboy.

"Playboy? No. You've saved me enough at the office to know that. However, I'm not a monk either," was his response.

I nodded. "What lonely, angry, sad, and gorgeous man with a strong libido wouldn't partake in casual sex now and again?"

He pursed his lips at me, his face unamused. "You see more than what's good for you."

"Like you?"

"Exactly."

I still didn't get it, why he didn't regard me the same as all the other women. Fuck and run, look but don't touch. I sighed and leaned back in my chair. What was it about me that attracted him?

"You're daydreaming again, Palmer," he said, bringing my mind back to the present. I looked around and noticed Tiffany was no longer hovering over his cock.

I gave him my best bitch brow to keep up the show. "Thinking, Thorne,"

"More fun if you were day dreaming."

"And why is that?"

He smirked at me and returned to his work, ignoring me.

A moment later my phone buzzed. Why couldn't he just *tell me*?

*Because if you were day dreaming, I would have a valid excuse to punish you for ignoring your work.*

*Oh, that's why.* I swallowed past the lump that had formed in my throat before responding.

*Okay, no more texting from you during work.*

Lame, but that was all I could come up with. My brain had exploded at the implications of his words, wildfire ripping its way through my body. How did he always do that to me?

*Telling me what I can and cannot do, Palmer? Now THAT'S something to punish you for.*

My jaw dropped as I stared at the tiny screen. He was going to be the death of me in the most glorious of ways.

I was startled out of my thoughts by an unexpected rapping on the door, making me jump.

"Hey guys," Mark, from the office next door, called from the entry. "Jack just called a meeting in Lincoln."

We both nodded and rose from our desks, heading to the south side of the floor where the company's largest conference room resided. Almost fifty people filtered into the space. Nathan and I ended up being shoulder-to-shoulder, leaning against the wall, as there were only twenty seats in the room.

My eyes scanned the faces of the room, and I did a double take at the man sitting next to Jack Holloway.

"Fuck." I hissed through gritted teeth. What was Andrew doing here?

Nathan jumped, taken back by my low outburst. "What?"

"This'll go over like a pregnant pole-vaulter." I directed his gaze to Andrew.

"What the hell is he doing here?" Venom laced his tone as he shot daggers at him.

"All right, everyone. Settle down," Jack's voice boomed out over the murmur of the crowd. "This won't take too long; soon you will be back to the mounting piles on your desk."

The crowd chuckled, while Nathan and I turned and raised an eyebrow at one another. We always had mounting piles; it would be a blessing to have the stack some of the other attorney's had awaiting them. Oh, wait, we did. The difference being we had a bit of *everyone's* work. It came with the territory, and I was happy to have it, instead of going to a court room any day like many in our office.

"As you're all aware, we've been down a team member since Stephen's departure late last year. Well, it's been over six months, and I think we've finally have found the right man for the job," Jack announced. "Some of you may remember the man to my right, he was once an intern here, and I would like your help in welcoming Andrew Carter to our ranks."

The crowd erupted in applause and the Boob-Squad already seemed to have Andrew in their sights.

"Andrew's first day will be tomorrow, and he'll need everyone's help getting reacquainted with Holloway and Holloway."

Andrew caught my gaze, and I stood, frozen. A huge grin spread on his face: he looked like such a cute, innocent kid when he did that.

"Hey, Lila!" Andrew called out, interrupting Jack.

My face heated up in embarrassment as everyone turned to see who he was looking at.

"Hi, Drew." I waved my hand, trying to move the room back to the topic at hand.

Nathan tensed beside me, but my eyes remained on Andrew, and I watched his flicker beside me to Nathan. His gaze hardened, but he kept the smile plastered on his face.

"Well, now that everyone knows Andrew and Delilah are acquainted…" Jack chuckled. "Let's get back to work."

With a clap of his hands, the mass dispersed to their separate sections of the office.

Just as I was making my way through the doorway, a hand grabbed my wrist and pulled me back. The sudden halt caused Nathan to crash into me. Andrew's strong arms wrapped around me and lifted me into the air, then back down for a hug. My eyes widened before I began laughing.

Nathan shot us an icy glare before continuing down the hall, and for some reason I found the sight hysterical. It made me laugh more, but everyone thought it was due to Andrew's antics. The exchange had been so quick; I figured no one had picked up on the cold undercurrent.

"Something about that guy rubs me the wrong way," Andrew said out of nowhere.

"He's harmless," I assured him. "By the way…what the hell are you doing here, and why didn't you tell me?"

A sheepish grin spread on his face. "I wanted it to be a surprise."

"Well, it worked."

"I hope you don't mind."

I gave him a knowing look. "Andrew, I know you loved working at Holloway and Holloway as much as Caroline and I did when we all interned together. You just chose the dark side."

"Well, I came back to become a real Jedi."

"Welcome back, Anakin," I said with a smile. "Well, I have a mountain and a half waiting for me."

I turned to head out the door when his voice stopped me.

"What was the name of that bar by your place? Skips? Tips?"

"Nipps," I responded.

"Later, Lila."

I waved back and headed in the direction of my office. Once there, the tension was rolling off Nathan, permeating our space. He didn't say anything for over an hour, and I could no longer stand the tension. I sent him a text hoping it would cure his foul mood.

*So, what was that about punishment? I'd like to hear more about that.*

He smirked at the message, and his shoulders dropped and relaxed.

The remainder of the day went off without a hitch as did the next day. Andrew was nowhere to be seen on Friday, his first official day, and I was thankful.

# CHAPTER 12

———⇒»»•◆•»»⇐———

"What's this?" Nathan asked as I handed him the jagged piece of metal.

"It's a key to my condo."

"I don't want it." He thrust his hand back toward me.

"Take the damn key," I said. We stood at a standstill, neither backing down. "Look, my neighbor is getting annoyed at the late night knocking, and we haven't spent a night apart in three weeks."

He contemplated my words for a moment, the warring indecision etched onto his features before he conceded. "Fine." Pulling his keys from his pocket he twisted the metal piece on to the key ring.

"Here," he said, holding his hand out to me.

"What?" I asked, confused.

"If I can molest you at all hours of the night at my will, you should be able to return the favor." He smirked as he placed his key in my open palm.

The next day, I yawned and rotated my shoulders, attempting to relieve some of the ache. I should have known not to tease Nathan; he'd made sure to prolong his own release to torment me.

The day was over and as soon as I entered my condo, I stripped out of my suit and into a sun dress with a shrug. It was a nice spring day, the temperature reaching into the mid-sixties, and I was excited for the coming warmth of summer. I located a pair of strappy sandals hiding in a corner of my closet before heading out the door and up to Nathan's to pick him up.

I told myself it was to pick him up, as if it was a date, something planned, but once again it was an unspoken thing we did together. I opened the door with my key and walked in.

It had been a difficult trade off, but in the end was a great idea. I felt safer not leaving my door unlocked, as did Nathan, and it came in handy when once, after a night of drinking, I realized I didn't have my keys with me.

I walked in and called out, my voice echoing on the empty walls and near vacant rooms. I sighed. Again, another reminder. He didn't care about furniture or decorations; his condo held the bare minimum. The only things on the walls were holes; he was up to seventeen, one more since yesterday. I told him he needed to get a punching bag; it was cheaper than drywall replacement.

I found him out on the terrace sitting on one of the lounge chairs, a cigarette between his lips. His leg was bouncing at near sonic speed, his fingers pulling at his hair. He screamed of nervous agitation, and I cried inside knowing the cause.

I walked forward and sat down next to him. "I didn't know you smoked."

His head tilted to me in acknowledgement as he took a long drag.

"Sometimes," he admitted as he released the smoke from his lungs.

"It bothers you that much...my feelings?" Brutal honesty wasn't our thing, but I wanted him to tell me.

"Yes," he responded after a moment. "I don't want you to feel that way."

I nodded in understanding. I hated it, but I had hoped he would open up to me.

After taking a deep breath, I sat down next to him and grabbed his arm. My thumb massaged the surgical scar on the inside of his wrist as I pulled his hand to me, and took a drag of his cigarette. It burned, but sparked an old craving. He was watching me in intense fascination.

"What?"

"I don't like the way he looks at you."

I was stunned at his declaration; it had a possessive edge about it.

"And?" I pressed.

His face twisted for a moment before a cocky smile presented itself. His hand moved between my thighs and grabbed my pussy, his fingers pushing the thin cotton of my panties against my opening.

"For me only," he snarled.

I shook my head and huffed. "You are such a fucking contradiction."

"What?"

"I wish I knew what was going on in that head of yours sometimes."

He shook his head as he leaned down to put the cigarette out on the concrete. "No, you don't. It's dark in here." He tapped on his skull.

With that, he stood. After offering me a hand up, we headed out to Nipps for our Friday relaxation.

Two hours later, we were laughing about who knows what, snacking on bar food and I was two beers in. I snagged the cigarette from between his fingers and took another puff.

"Delilah Anne Palmer!" I heard my name yelled out from somewhere in the bar. I turned to find Andrew staring at me as he stomped over. "Smoking? You worked so hard to quit, and now you're at it again?"

I sighed, my body sagging. "It was just a drag, Andrew."

"A gateway drag."

I glared up at him. "What are you doing here?"

He pulled the bar stool out from beside me and sat down.

He signaled to John, the bartender. "Well I was thinking we could have a celebratory drink."

"Whatever," Nathan muttered from my other side.

Andrew peeked around me and his face dropped. "What are you doing here?"

Nathan quirked his eyebrow at Andrew's tone. "It's Friday night, this is the closest bar to my house, and I needed a drink."

"Cool. Just stay away from Lila."

"Andrew!" I shrieked.

Nathan's body stiffened. "What did you say?" He shifted, starting to stand.

Andrew's body shifted as well, both ready to get up and beat the shit out of one another. "You heard me. You're bad news, I can tell."

Nathan sneered at him. "What the hell do you know about me? Nothing. So shut the fuck up."

Andrew stood. "I've seen the way you look at her. Stay the fuck away."

"What way do I 'look' at her?" Nathan asked, mirroring Andrew's movement.

"Like she's another notch to add to your bed post."

I had to place my hand in front of my mouth to keep from spitting my beer out at Andrew's comment.

I stood between them, a hand pressed to each of their chests. "All right, boys, back up."

Andrew backed down, returning to his seat. Nathan was still standing, but he took a step back.

"I have to go to the bathroom; do you think you two can be civilized?"

"Don't worry," Nathan began, tilting the bottle back and downed the remaining contents of his bottle. "I'm on my way out."

I couldn't believe my non-boyfriend and my ex were fighting over me. I hated watching Nathan go, but tried to remain unfazed by it.

"I don't trust him," Andrew said.

I sighed. "He's fine, really."

"I'm surprised to see you two out together. Word is you can't stand each other."

I nodded in agreement. "Word is correct. Like he said, it's the closest bar to our building, and it's Friday night. We've run into one another here before."

"I still don't like him."

118

I rolled my eyes and excused myself, leaving Andrew at the bar as I headed to the restroom. Just as I placed my hand on the door to push it open, someone grabbed my arm and pulled me in. I didn't have to look to know who it was. His grip moved down to my waist as he turned me to face him, his lips attacking mine. We walked backward, and I stopped when I met a barrier behind me that I assumed was the sink.

My body was buzzing, high on the feeling of him being so close. Heat coursed through me, lighting up every nerve-ending in a way only he could do.

The hands at my waist tightened their grip and lifted me onto the counter with ease. My legs spread open, wrapping around his waist, welcoming him between my thighs. His fingers moved to the hem of my dress, pushing the fabric up to my hips. He leaned forward. His cock was straining against his pants when he pushed into my now wet center. One of my hands fisted in his hair; the other kept me upright, pushing against the counter and his body.

His mouth moved down my neck and above where it met my shoulder; he bit me hard. A shiver ran down my spine, and I was pooling between my legs as he clamped and sucked harder.

"But you left," I managed to pant out.

His teeth detached from my skin, his tongue lapping at the new mark. "I couldn't exactly follow you into the bathroom to fuck your brains out with your knight in shining armor watching, now could I?"

His fingers worked between us, pulling my panties to the side, and then he plunged two fingers inside. I moaned at the feeling, while I was kissing up and down his neck, my tongue tasting his skin.

He let out a low, dark chuckle. "Already this wet for me? That's my good little slut," he whispered in my ear.

I cried out as his fingers flexed upward, hitting my G-Spot.

"Shh!" he hissed then changed to taunting. "I'm going to fuck you. Here. Now. And you're going to come so hard around my cock while you hold in your screams."

I shook my head, knowing Andrew would come if he heard.

He pulled his fingers from me, brought them to my lips, and pushed them into my mouth.

"Suck." I did as he ordered, lapping up my juices from each finger, and he continued to dictate how it was going to go, "So fucking sexy like that. You love it when I tell you what to do; how to be my good little whore. Now tell me… Do you taste good?"

I nodded in agreement, my eyes transfixed on him. I watched him lick his lips, his eyes fixed on my mouth. I made sure my tongue made more than one appearance, teasing him in the process.

The telltale sounds of his belt being loosened, and the clicking of the metal teeth of a zipper, filled my ears. He forced the rest of his fingers between my lips as he pulled his fucking perfect cock out and tapped the head against my clit. I moaned at the sensation, like the wanton slut I felt like with him. He teased my slit, slipping the tip up and down, but not entering.

With his fingers in my mouth, he grabbed hold of my jaw and nipped on the spot just behind my ear. "Remember to keep quiet, baby. You don't want anyone barging in, do you? At least not until I've gotten mine and filled you up with my come."

I shook my head, my body tingling in anticipation. I had never done anything like that in my life, but I would do anything he asked of me.

In one swift motion, he was buried inside me, just as he had said. My teeth clamped down on his fingers to keep the scream in, but my body still let out a sob of pleasure, the whimper slipping out. His hips rocked, pushing his cock in and pulling it back out. In with a hard thrust and out as fast.

The hand that wasn't knuckle deep in my mouth was gripping my ass like a vice as his cock pistoned into me.

"This is your fault. Fucking flirting with another guy in front of me, practically offering up your pussy to him. But it's not yours to give away, is it?" he asked in a condescending tone.

His fingers were still lodged in my mouth, rendering me unable to respond, but I managed to get out an almost "no."

"That's right, baby, it's not. Your fucking pussy belongs to me, and I'm going to make sure everyone knows that it's taken."

My head was foggy as he pounded into me. I couldn't tell which way was up. I didn't care we were in a dirty bar bathroom, or that people could probably hear us. All I cared about was him and the way he made my body sing. Only for him.

"Oh, shit! Baby, I'm so close," he grunted. "Are you close?"

I hummed around his fingers, my eyes locked on his.

"That's what I thought."

He smirked before pulling out. I cried out at the sudden loss, almost sobbing as I had been a few strokes away from my orgasm.

"On your knees," he commanded, tugging on my jaw, drawing me down from the counter.

Once I was kneeling in front of him, the fingers in my mouth moved to my hair. He grabbed a fistful of my locks and yanked my head back so I was looking up at him, my jaw going slack from the angle. His breath was erratic as he smacked his cock against my bottom lip, the tip running across my lips and cheeks.

"You like that? Fucking dirty girl. Look at you, fucking me in the bathroom of a bar then begging to suck my cock."

His fist pumped his shaft at a furious pace. He relaxed his motions and tilted his hips forward, pushing the head to my lips. I began sucking on the tip, licking anywhere I could, tasting myself on him. His eyes were dark and glazed as he stared down at me.

Pulling harder on my hair, he detached my lips from his dick. His stroking resumed, letting the tip bounce on my lower lip. His fingers flexed around my hair, holding me in place. His whole body tensed and his face screwed up in a look of pain. A strangled cry left his lips as I felt the first warm drops hit my lips and cheek.

He repositioned it so the next few streams landed on my chest and neck. His eyes were hooded as he freed my hair and used his hand and cock to move his come around on my skin. He had a loopy grin on his face as he rubbed it in, all over my neck, and any exposed parts of my chest. Even the come on my face he rubbed in until it was all dry.

I licked my lips to get the drops that had landed, tasting his salty tang. It was obvious he liked that, and placed his cock in front of my mouth. I greedily sucked him in, making sure to get all of the remaining fluid.

"What was that all about?" I asked as I released him.

He smirked as he pulled his pants back up and tucked everything back into place. "Now you smell like me."

"What?"

He leaned down, nipping at my ear lobe. "When you go back out there, any guy who comes close will smell my jizz on you."

My eyes widened, and heat rose on my skin. I righted my clothing and turned to check the mirror. My eyes were bright, my skin flushed, and my pussy twitched, still aching for release.

"Have fun, Honeybear," he said with a wink, a kiss to my forehead, and slap on my ass as he walked back out the door.

Once he left, I pulled out a paper towel from the dispenser and got it wet. I worked to clean the come off my jaw, chin, and cheeks, but stopped there. The paper towels were empty and it was everywhere. I hoped it wasn't as noticeable as he implied, and sighed in defeat; he'd won after all.

My gaze returned to the mirror as I readjusted my dress and hair. After a moment of trying to calm down, I decided I didn't look like I had just been fucked and headed back out to the bar.

"About time, I was about to send in a rescue crew," Andrew joked when I returned to my seat.

"Sorry, I…really had to go." The lie seemed apparent, even to my own ears. It was then that I realized I never did get to use the restroom the way I had intended.

"Okay…"

We started to chat about his first day and how it went. It had been enjoyable enough. He was happy to have left Lerner, Sorenson, and Martin, and return to Holloway and Holloway. He lamented having turned down their offer during our internship together.

My pussy was still begging for release, and I wondered if it was like blue balls for men. I was crawling out of my skin. I needed to leave. I needed to find Nathan and yell at him for leaving me in such a state before I fucked his brains out into the morning.

Drew leaned in to say something, his face inches from mine when he said the unimaginable. "What's that smell?"

"Smell?" I questioned. My nerves were shot. *Please, no. Please, no.*

Andrew sniffed around. "Yeah, well, you wouldn't notice. It smells like…" He leaned closer to whisper in my ear. "It smells like come."

It was my turn for my eyes to widen. My mouth dropped open in disbelief that Nathan had been correct. Men *could* smell him.

"I…well… It is a dive bar."

Andrew stared at me. "Don't tell me it's coming from you." Silence surrounded us, and I had no idea how to respond. "Is that what took you so long in the bathroom? Letting some random guy get his rocks off all over you?"

My embarrassment switched to anger. I did *not* like his implications. "You know what, Andrew, what I do is no longer any of your concern."

Andrew's eyes darted around the bar, looking for the guilty party. "So my friend getting fucked in a bathroom by some stranger is none of my concern? Who *is* the cock sucker?"

"Technically, I'm the cock sucker." I gave him a sweet smile. "Just so you know it wasn't some random guy. I don't need you to come in here and play big brother, or knight. It's my business, not yours."

With that I stood, threw a twenty on the bar and walked out.

I walked home as fast as my legs would carry me and stepped into an awaiting elevator. My fingers hit the button for the fourteenth floor over and over in my agitation. After a few minutes, I arrived at his door and began pounding. I was not going to use my key; he was coming to me.

It took him a moment to get the door opened and when it did, he stared at me in surprise.

I launched myself at him, pushing him against the wall as the door clicked closed behind me. "You, sir, are a fucking bastard."

# CHAPTER 13

My fists clenched in the fabric of his shirt, my gaze glaring. I couldn't believe all that had happened in the last hour. It was unbelievable what he had done and that Andrew could smell it on me. I was so embarrassed and pissed...and still turned on. I had to be a sick pervert.

"What the fuck was that all about?"

He smirked in that damned way he always did.

"He noticed." It wasn't a question, it was a statement. He leaned down to whisper in my ear. "Good."

His hands moved to grab my ass, pulling me against his body.

My hand smacked against his chest. "I can't fucking believe you."

"You're the one who said you were mine," he said, throwing my words back at me. "I was just making it known."

I pushed out of his arms and stepped back, regarding him warily. His arms crossed in front of his chest, closing himself off. "You're always trying to push me away, but I want you to think about it. I mean really think about me no longer being around… or better yet, me with another man, screaming out *his* name as *his* cock is buried in me. Tell me, what do you *think* now?"

I watched his face contort as he did what I asked. The usual myriad of emotions flickered across his face, but then there was a softness I'd never seen before, and it made him look very different.

In a split second, he snatched hold of my wrist and pulled me to him. His eyes widened and his gaze shot down to his hand, staring in absolute disbelief. It had been impulse. The moment he thought about me with another man, his possessive side came out.

His hand relaxed and as it began to drop, I slid mine into his. His eyes grew in alarm, his breath picking up in tempo.

"Shh," I soothed, my thumb running over his in small circles. His eyes looked tormented, tearing at me. The simple gesture of affection was almost too much for him.

My gaze flickered to a hole in the wall next to his head that had not been there before we went out. It was out of place, on the opposite side of the foyer from the others.

"Did you punch another hole in the wall?" I questioned. "Were you angry that you let yourself go again and showed me the real you?" His face became steel, like he didn't want to admit I was right. "Did you do that because you were pissed at taking me in a public restroom or because you claimed me as yours?"

All expression on his face fell away.

"What does it matter?" he asked in almost a sigh of defeat.

126

"What does it *matter*?" I mimicked. "We've been going with the flow and then all of the sudden... I don't get you."

"You're the one who wants to 'be.' I told you it was a bad idea," he spat. He picked up a glass from the table next to the door that contained a small amount of amber colored liquid and tipped it against his lips.

"Yes, but your actions back at the bar? Laying claim to me caveman style? Being possessive and jealous?" He stared at me in disbelief as the words began to match up in his mind, showing him what he'd done. "You changed things."

His gaze snapped back to me and the painful expression looked like it turned to fear then anger. His arm swung out, throwing the glass in his hand into the wall. It shattered into tiny pieces as he yelled out. I jumped at his sudden aggression, surprised by his actions.

"Fuck!" His hands tugged at his hair. "Why was he there?"

"*Who*? Andrew?" I was confused, wondering what Andrew had to do with anything.

"He doesn't know shit about me!" His lips twitched and his nostrils flared.

"Well, he seems to think he knows *something*."

"With all the rumors, he probably believed them. He seems the type."

"Before I touch that last part...what rumors?"

That stopped him cold and he turned to stare at me. "Lila, you're intelligent, so I know you've figured out transactional law and contracts are not my area, but I can do it."

I nodded. "You don't have the personality and no one graduates with honors from Harvard Law to work contracts at a law firm in Indianapolis, albeit a large one."

"Exactly."

There was a pause, his hand moving through his hair, tugging at the chestnut strands. His jaw clenched, his forehead crinkled, as if lost in thought.

"The last few years…hell, they've been hell…" He trailed off and began pacing in front of me. His other hand moved to his chest, fisting the fabric above his heart. "I can't go through that pain again. If I love you, then that's something they can take away from me. Take revenge on me by hurting you. I can't deal with that." His voice dropped to a whisper, so low I almost couldn't make out what he said. "Not again."

My heart thudded in my chest when he mentioned even the prospect of loving me; admitting to both of us that it was a possibility.

He stopped and turned back to me, closing the distance. He surprised me; his lips attacked my mouth, his tongue forcing its way in to mix with mine. There was desperation in his actions. His arms wrapped around me, pulling me to him. Our need was fierce, pushing and pulling.

He slowed his kisses. They became lighter, almost savoring. He leaned back, his hand reached up, caressing my cheek with the backs of his fingers.

"I'm not worried about you being hurt by me, Lila. I'm worried about you being hurt *because* of me."

He was soft and tender for the briefest of moments. Even that seemed too much for him and his expression turned pained, and then the pacing resumed.

He stopped with his back facing me, and I watched a shudder move through him; from his head down his spine. His agitation seeped out, infecting me.

I took my bottom lip between my teeth, my fingers knotted and fidgeted at my waist. My whole body was shaking; my chest constricted, hindering my ability to breathe.

We were the same.

Broken.

His pacing resumed, and I heard him mumbling, but I couldn't make out the words. For a brief moment, I feared for his sanity. His chest expanded in deep hard breaths. I couldn't tell what emotion would face me as they were all present, and the anxiety in the room continued to grow. He turned and stopped in front of me. His nostrils flared, his eyes wide, and I took an involuntary small step back, my body bending away from him. His gaze ran up and down my body, taking me in.

"You think being a federal prosecutor is great. You work hard to put heinous criminals away, hopefully for good. You don't think about the repercussions. About how the ones you're prosecuting or their families may be angry with you and want revenge for you trying to uphold the law and make people safe. You don't think about how someone will try to take your life because they blame you for ruining their life or their loved ones. They don't care who else gets hurt in their quest to get to you. Sometimes they even threaten them to scare you." His manic pacing resumed.

After a moment, he headed to the living room and sat down on the couch. His eyes were fixed on the fireplace, his leg bouncing at a furious pace. He picked up a sandstone coaster from the coffee table and twirled it in his hand.

I moved to stand near him, remaining silent so he would continue. A snarl ripped through his chest as his arm pulled back and he chucked the coaster into the fireplace. It fractured, sending dust and debris around the room.

"I was cocky. I thought nothing and no one could touch me. I was very wrong." His eyes were glassy and his voice wooden.

The weight of all his words dropped me to the ground in front of him. A tear escaped and landed on the carpet between us. There was more, so much more he was omitting.

"I couldn't do it anymore. I couldn't handle it, not after... I tried, I did. I failed miserably when not even a month back in, I exploded in the court room."

His eyes met mine. His look was pleading, begging me for understanding.

"But you're not a prosecutor anymore," I observed.

"Do you think that matters, Lila?" he asked. "This condo? It isn't even under my name. Because I'm still alive."

There was a shift, and calmness took hold of him. It was eerie, and I assumed it was from years of hiding from everyone. He just flipped the switch and that was it. Topic ended.

His gaze bored into mine, and I felt oddly exposed. It was like he was opening me up, seeing everything that I was…or wasn't.

"Why are *you* so empty?" he asked.

I stared at him, stunned.

"I can see it as clear as day. It's one of the many things that drew me to you. You're empty. You wear a mask to hide it, to make yourself seem somewhat normal, but your face… Do you know how expressionless it is when you think no one is looking? I provoke you to get some kind of reaction, like you provoke me to feel. Have you ever been happy?"

I was bombarded with question after question, and my anxiety started clawing its way through my being.

"Is that why you chose law? Contracts in general, because it's cold with precise guidelines? The people at the office don't see it. They think you're frigid, but I know you have a loving soul. The problem is you were never shown love, right? That's very cruel, to grow up without love," he stated with a cool tone, his eyebrow quirked in curiosity.

"Shut up!" I jumped to my feet, my fists clenched at my sides, my eyes blazing. I felt like a cat; the hackles standing on my neck, baring my teeth as I hissed. It was like he was poking me with a stick, and I wanted to swat at him to get him to stop.

He stood and walked over to stand directly in front of me. "Why? Because you don't want someone to point out what you're lacking? That's why things failed with you and Andrew, isn't it? He couldn't take your darkness, couldn't fill your void. He seems like the type to want to fix something that's broken."

"Shut up, shut up, shut up!" I screamed, my fists beating against his chest.

He needed to stop, I needed him to stop. How? How did he know what no one else knew?

*I can't stand to look at you.*

*No one will ever want you. No one will ever love you.*

*I hate you. I never wanted you. I was dumped with you.*

*You. Are. Nothing.*

"Please, it hurts!" I moaned, my heart shredding inside me.

"Why?"

"Because I was never wanted, I was never good enough, never smart enough, never loved! He *hated* me; I was in the way of his happiness, shackled to him."

Their words were running through my mind on a loop. All of the things they had said to me my whole life.

*I wish you'd never been born.*

*No one wants you here, you should just leave.*

"He hated that my mother died and forced me upon him: a child he never wanted from a woman he knew for a day. The things he said, the looks he gave...so many times, he wouldn't even give me that. It hurt more than when he smacked me or grabbed me and yelled. Those were the only times he ever touched me. He was my father. He was supposed to love me. *Protect* me!" My chest felt like it was ripping as I spilled my darkest secrets, showing him just how much I was lacking.

His face was pale, but there was no abhorrent look of pity—more like an expression of understanding and empathy. So, I took a deep breath and braced myself so I could continue on.

"My stepmother, she ignored me. Oh, God...the nasty things she would say to bring me down. She knew he wouldn't stop her; he encouraged her. Then there was Adam..." I paused, but wasn't sure I could find the words to describe him. I shivered as I envisioned him, sneering at me. My whole body shook with violent vibrations.

"He took high advantage of being able to say and do what-ever he wanted. He hated it when I moved in, hated his beloved stepfather bringing him a sister, and made it his personal mission to make me the most alienated and bullied kid in school. I kept my head down, my mouth shut, and prayed for someone to see me. For someone to love me... I still don't know why I never killed myself. I thought about it, a lot."

My voice was cracking at the end; I couldn't take anymore. It felt like my chest had been cut open, and my worthless self had been laid bare for Nathan to see, to dissect, and then to abandon as a lost cause. I wouldn't blame him, because everything he said was true. I was hollow, nothing but emptiness. I so craved the love I had been denied and the chance to love in return. Words could not express how deeply I craved the feeling of being *wanted*.

Nathan did that. He made me feel what I hadn't ever felt before: wanted, desired, beautiful, sexy. To him, I was all of those. He made me start to think all I'd been led to believe was a lie. He was filling the void. I would give him anything he wanted. It was twisted and unhealthy, but I didn't care. My feelings for him were more than I had ever felt for anyone in my life.

Sobs wracked my body, my fists losing their momentum. His arms wrapped around me, pulling me to him, holding me up.

His fingers stroked my hair, calming me. "You're dead inside, just like me."

"That's not true," I argued. "You have very strong emotions, violent almost."

He laughed. It was almost maniacal. "You don't get it." He pulled back to look at me, his gaze serious and intense. My muscles tensed in response. "I wish I was dead." I stared up at him in disbelief. "I wish the paramedics had taken five more minutes to get there."

Without thought, my hand reached up and connected with his cheek. It was as involuntary as him grabbing my wrist. I couldn't stand the mere thought of him not being there with me. His head snapped back to face me. He wasn't angry, but stunned instead. Tears slid down my cheeks.

"Please, don't leave me," I whispered, my voice breaking.

"I wish the battery on the defibrillator had been out," he continued on; the emotion gone from his face and voice. "That way they wouldn't have been able to restart my heart. Because then I wouldn't feel dead inside, in pain daily. Because I wouldn't be here, hurting you."

He paused in thought for a moment, probably asking himself how much he could give.

"I'm angry because I'm alive. My heart, my soul...they're gone, dead, but my body remains. This is my purgatory."

Tears were streaming down my face even faster. My fists picked up their beating against his chest.

"No, no, no, no! Please, please, Nathan... I can't fathom... I *need* you. You make... I'm falling... Please, please, please." I begged and pleaded over and over again. For what, I didn't even know; for him to stay with me, for him to live, for him to never wish to be dead and to be with me always. I *needed* him to live.

I couldn't even make out what I was saying, but I hoped he understood the meaning. I was falling, hard, for him. My chest constricted, and I almost doubled over from the strain. The feeling was so foreign I didn't know what to do.

His arms wrapped tighter around me in an attempt to contain me, but I pulled back. My hands smacked his away, hitting his chest.

"No!" I screamed, pushing him away.

I didn't want him to soothe me. Not anymore. If he didn't want to stay there with me, what was the point?

"Lila," he cried out, clearly stunned at my reaction. I could hear the desperation in his tone, panic setting in. His hands grabbed at my arms. "Baby, stop!"

"No!"

Every time he tried to restrain me, I escaped. Through my blurry eyes, I saw his panic mixed with anger and frustration.

He managed to get a hold of my wrists and walk me backward into the wall, pinning me.

He growled, his forehead resting against mine. "Calm down."

"Say it!"

His eyes were screwed tight, knowing what I was asking; his fists closed around my hair as he took in a shuddered breath.

"I want you," he said before capturing my lips with his.

# CHAPTER 14

He leaned over me, pressing me into the wall. Our lips, teeth, and tongues met in a frenzy I had never experienced. I pushed back into him, my fingers reached into his silky locks and pulled hard, tipping his head back. He groaned as our lips broke apart, his hips rocking against mine. He was ready, very ready.

My teeth nipped at his jaw, working down to his neck. I found a nice spot right below his ear, and bit down, sucking, marking him.

"Fuck." His hands moved down to my hips, his fingers digging in to the flesh beneath.

I growled at him like a possessed demon. "Jesus... I can't take it! You're mine. You're not going anywhere. *Mine*!"

"Why do I matter? What difference, if any, do I make?" His words spurred me on; gasoline on my raging fire.

I'd show him and then some. I'd tell him why we needed each other, but without words.

I pulled his hair in my fist, smashed his lips to mine one more time and shoved him toward the bedroom.

"Lie down," I ordered.

I had no idea what I was doing, but that was the point. Thoughts were always getting in our way, keeping us from going anywhere. I needed that blinding white, all-consuming rapture we shared to engulf us, to wipe our minds clean like it always did. In that place, I not only felt whole, I felt powerful.

He stripped off his clothes, his eyes shifting down to his eternal erection. I wasted no time tearing my clothes off, and pushed him down on the bed. I'd show him why he couldn't leave me and why we both mattered.

I climbed on top of him, straddling his legs. His cock was so hard, lying against his stomach. Hard and angry. Beautiful. I wanted to taste him, but my need to ride him was winning. I had to have him inside me.

I slid my hand down over the head of his dick, spreading the pre-cum around. My hips rocked, sliding my pussy over his length.

I grabbed his cock and squeezed it.

"Power…you think you wield it with this? It's what makes you feel alive?" It was rhetorical. He blinked as if in understanding of what I meant then stared deep in my eyes, his lips parted, his breathing soft. "That's not a power that can be sustained. But this," I pointed to my heart, "this doesn't end, doesn't run out. This is true power. But you already know that, don't you? You've just forgotten how to use it."

His indifference was dwindling and he was listening with rapt attention.

"You want to know why you matter?"

"No, I don't care about that shit." His voice wavered.

"For a lawyer, you suck at lying." I dipped my head down and bit his bottom lip then dragged my hands up his forearms and pinned them above his head. "You matter because…"

I left him hanging. He did that to me all the time. I'd let him figure it out.

I reached over and grabbed the tie he was wearing earlier, having thrown it on the bed as he had undressed. Without skipping a beat, I wound it around his hands and secured them nice and tight to the post.

"You're not going anywhere. You're going to watch me fuck you while you figure out why either of us matter. Why we feel like this when we're together. Suck it up and watch me take what's mine."

I stood from my position and turned away from him, bent over, spreading my legs so he could see all I had to offer. My hands wound through my legs to my entrance, my fingers teasing along the slit. I could feel my juices dripping.

"Shit," he ground out through is teeth. I could hear him struggling to break free, so he could take me hard and fast the way we both needed it. Not tonight.

"Andrew used to touch me here," I said, torturing him as I slipped my middle finger in.

He snarled at me. "I don't want to hear that!" I could hear the venom in his bite.

"Don't listen then. I'll show you." I continued on. My fingers dragged in and out, over and over again. Then I splayed them and didn't say a word, letting him think what he wanted as I dragged my juices up to my back entrance to tease him.

"That's mine. No one has touched you there, and no one will but me." His tone was beyond lethal. His breathing picked up and his hips bucked toward me.

The bed started rocking as he thrashed around, trying to break free, to grab me. There was a pitiful desperation in the sounds coming from him—from his moans, groans and whimpers, and I almost considered letting him go... *almost.*

"Think what you want," I mewled at him as my finger parted my cheeks and pushed in.

"Fucking untie me now!"

I peeked over my shoulder to find him seething. A shudder ran through me, and I licked my lips, continuing on.

We were both lashing out. He wasn't the only one in pain. But unlike him, I kept fighting, kept going. He'd already given up. When we touched...it all clicked into place. He was my soul mate; I could feel it when he was near. Our bodies together made sense; our lives on a whole had new meaning. We were no longer condemned to walk alone like the undead.

"Quit being so cold to me," I said. "We want each other... because..."

I waited for him to fill in the blanks as I continued to finger my ass.

"I don't know...fucking Christ! I have no idea." He sounded completely broken.

Hearing him break down was painful but there was beauty in his surrender.

I relented; released my power play and sat back down, straddling his chest.

"You do know. We both know. When you realize why we belong together...you'll quit relying on old habits and pretending that you have no purpose, no direction." I kissed him hard and his whole body arched toward me.

His body clung to mine, even though his hands were not free to join in.

"There's peace in the blackness. We've found it. I'm beginning to embrace it." I tried explaining it to him in simple terms as I scooted down his waist, stopping when I felt his hot head against my clit.

His eyes closed, shutting me out along with the inevitable pain of allowing himself to love me. "Please! Stop this."

"Won't admit it out loud? Fine. I'll just make you feel it." I slid against him, moaning at the feeling of his silky hard length as it rubbed against my entrance and my clit.

"Shit, baby!" His eyes scrunched tighter, hips pushing up into mine. "I can feel how fucking wet you are for me."

I slid back up and lined the tip up before gliding down, taking him to the hilt. My eyes screwed tight, my mouth dropping open, a guttural moan escaping me as he filled me. My fingers flexed, pushing my nails into his chest.

"Oh, God. Fuck, Nathan!" I shuddered as he flexed his hips up, his feet gaining purchase to help prop him up.

My body began acting on its own, sliding up and down his hard cock, taking him as deep as I could. I cried out every time I slammed all the way down and whimpered when I retreated.

The pace picked up, my body bouncing up and down as I rode him, as I took control.

"You look so fucking good riding me." His eyes were clouded, jaw slack. "I love watching my cock disappear in you. Do you like that, too, baby? I bet you do. You're a good little cock whore that way."

I cried out. "Fuck, Nathan!"

"That's it, scream my name. Shit, I want to touch you, baby."

At that I stopped, and sat on him for a moment before standing up with a smirk and looking down at him.

"Shit, don't stop!"

His hips were moving of their own volition, seeking my pussy out with desperate thrusts. I licked my lips; he was delectable in that state of lust. My fingers moved back inside of myself, pumping in and out, torturing him. Nathan panting, muscles tight... I almost came just from the sight alone.

I turned around and sat back down, reverse cowgirl, taking him inside my pussy again. My wet fingers moved back to my puckered hole, now on display for him. I pushed one finger in to tease him, then another, stretching it open right in his line of sight.

"Fuck, fuck, fuck!"

"See something you like?" My fingers moved in and out at a slow pace.

I could feel my muscles coiling. With each thrust up and downward fall, I was being driven closer and closer to the edge.

Up. Down. In. Out.

"You are such a fucking naughty little slut. I will fucking pound you so hard in your ass. I take what's mine, and your sweet ass is mine," he growled, thrusting hard into me.

I shuddered at his words. They sent a fire racing through my body, and I fell over the edge. My head was tilted back, and I screamed his name, unable to move as I clenched around him.

I heard the sound of wood splintering before I felt his hands on me, grabbing me, pushing my body, bending it to his will. He had broken free and flipped us to where my chest was pressed into the mattress, my ass up in the air, and his cock still buried to the hilt. His fingers twisted in my hair, pushing my head down while his other arm pinned the hand that had been teasing my ass, against my back.

He wasted no time and began thrusting, pushing me harder into the bed. A relentless pounding.

"Such a damn fucking tease. Take it. Take my fucking cock."

I screamed out, my body burning. I hadn't even had the chance to come down before he was pushing me into another orgasm. My mouth was open, crying out in pleasure, sobbing from it.

"That's it, baby. Scream; tell me how much you love my cock buried in your tight pussy. Ungh," he grunted.

His pace was constant, furious; he wasn't letting up, and I wasn't coming down.

He released me and my arm; my head relaxed into the bed.

"Are you ready for it?" he asked. He disappeared from my back, and the sound of a drawer opening, followed by a familiar snap, was all I could hear over my harsh breaths. Cool liquid hit the heated skin above my pussy, and his cock popped out, sliding up the crack between my cheeks, wetting it. "Not that it matters, because I'm going to fuck your sweet ass regardless."

I tried to relax when I felt him push in. He went slow, letting me adjust to the odd feeling of being so full. He slid in all of the way and once there, he leaned forward, his mouth at my ear.

"Mine. All fucking mine, baby."

"Yours," I agreed.

One arm wrapped around my waist, his fingers ghosting their way down to my eager pussy. The other came around my chest and lifted my body up, bringing my back against his chest. His hand moved up, his fingers wrapping around my neck, but pushing down against my collar bone. His other hand moved down and slid two fingers in, the palm of his hand pressing into my clit.

Once he was ready, he pulled his hips back only to slide back in. It was a slower, sensual, punishing pace. His fingers slid into my pussy at the same time his cock filled my ass.

"Baby, God, your fucking ass loves my cock, doesn't it? Yeah, all of you loves my cock. I could fuck you all day long. So fucking sexy."

My arms reached behind me, grabbing onto his hair, tugging.

"Nathan…shit, I love your cock!" I was shaking, with each thrust as I grew closer to another orgasm.

"Getting close again? Fucking naughty girl, so sexy when you come."

He licked up the side of my neck; his teeth scraping against my skin. I whimpered, my body shuddering, a silent scream building on my lips as my orgasm ripped through me, making me clench around his cock and fingers.

"That's it baby. Shit, fucking come…oh fuck!"

His fingers closed around my neck, squeezing as his muscles tensed before he exploded inside me.

His body relaxed, his strength giving out, and we fell to the bed. His arms were still wrapped around me, one hand at my chest, the other cupping my sex.

We laid there for a moment to catch our breaths. His lips ghosted across my neck, his tongue peeking out to taste.

"Mine," he whispered.

I turned my head to look behind me, my body twisting in his arms. I pressed my lips to his and he leaned forward to deepen the kiss, his arms pulling me tighter to him.

"Mine," I whispered in return.

He took a deep shuddering breath before pulling the blanket over us and sending us into what would hopefully be a peaceful sleep.

# CHAPTER 15

*I*t was dark, midnight black. Everything was. It always was. It was my room, but it wasn't...not anymore; it hadn't been for a long time. It was sparse. Empty. Nothing on the walls, not even color. Blank.

A dream or a nightmare; I didn't know which.

I heard...nothing. It was safe to move. I exited the room, my feet sliding across the hardwood.

I stumbled through the dark; my hands found the wall and I followed it to the open space of the living room. An eerie glow appeared, shining through the window, illuminating little, but it wasn't enough to create shadows.

They moved against the wall, sending shivers through me.

I knew the place, or I had known it. It had been many years since I was last here. Since I last saw...

*"Dad..."*

Slap!

*My head was flung to the side, my body twisting with the momentum, my hand slapping against the wall to keep me upright. My eyes opened, but I kept looking down. I turned my head as slow as possible. I started shaking more and more as my gaze inched upwards. Before I could see what was in front of me, I felt breath caress my skin; hot and heavy. A scathing voice spoke into my ear.*

*"Don't look at me. Keep your fucking eyes down. I can't stand to see you looking at me."*

*I complied, not wanting to anger him further.*

*"I told you. No one will ever love you."*

*I heard another familiar voice, not far away.*

*The first figure backed away. "You disgust me. Looking just like her with my eyes."*

*I heard footsteps grow closer. There was a slamming on either side of my head, and I cowered, the tears already stinging my eyes for what was to come.*

*"You are still such a stupid fucking girl," he growled, inches from my face.*

Adam.

*I continued to look down, hoping my silence would stay him.*

*"Everyone hates you. You should just fucking leave."*

*"The moment you turn eighteen, you are gone. I don't have to support your sorry ass anymore." Dad's voice called from somewhere in the darkness.*

*"Hear that? Gone," my stepmother, Cheryl, spat. "Maybe if you spread those prude legs of yours and take someone in, they'll let you stay with them. I hear virgins can fetch a*

*high price. Just throw a bag over your head, that way they won't have to look at your pathetic face. Because you are pathetic."*

*There was a reprieve, a short silence before Adam's hot breath was in my ear. "Do you think he will ever love you? You know the answer; it's no. How could he? You have nothing to offer him but your pussy."*

"Please, stop," I begged.

*I tilted my head up to meet his eyes; they were as black as obsidian. He glared down at me, snarling, and his body was shaking. He was the meanest son of a bitch to ever come near me.*

*His head flew back in laughter; full of menace and hate. To my horror, I watched as his black hair turned brown, and when his eyes returned to mine, Nathan's sea-blue's glared back, bright and menacing.*

*"They're right. Do you honestly think you can 'fix' me and that I'll love you, Lila?"*

*My eyes dropped back to the ground. I was shaking, hard. My chest was too tight.*

"Lila…"

*"How could I ever love you?"*

"Lila…"

*My whole body was moving; my stomach clenching. I felt like I was going to be sick.*

*"Look at me and then look at yourself. Do you really think someone like me could ever be with someone like you?"*

"Lila…"

*The shaking continued, rattling my body back and forth.*

"Lila!"

My eyes snapped wide open. Light greeted me, and I found myself staring straight into blue; Nathan's eyes. His real eyes, bright and full of worry.

The darkness was gone.

My stomach turned, and the bile was rising up, escaping. I kicked off the covers and rolled to the side, pushing my body up from the bed. I could still hear him calling to me as I attempted to run.

In my haste and dizziness, I began stumbling, almost falling to the ground. I managed to pick myself up before I went crashing to the floor. I made it to the bathroom, and reached the toilet. My retching echoed off the walls as I heaved the bile and acid flying from my stomach.

Dry heaves racked me, my body attempting to expunge the dream, to purge it from my mind and soul. Every part of me was shaking, and it took a moment to gain the strength to stand.

Years. It had been years since I had a nightmare like that: intense, real, terrifying. The magnitude was so great my body attempted to rid itself of the images, of the words. I sat on the floor in front of the toilet, while my breathing regulated. My heart was hammering against my chest, beating furiously in an attempt to escape.

Flee. Everything in me wanted to flee.

I could feel his eyes on me: watching, observing, and waiting. I didn't want him to see me in such a pathetic state. Vulnerability was a weakness I could not afford to show. It would be just another reason for him to leave me—another thing that would be too much for him to handle.

After a few minutes, I could breathe again, and I pulled myself from the floor. It wasn't an easy task with my body still shaking and my legs still feeling like limp noodles from our previous night's activities. I wobbled a bit before inching to the sink and grabbing my toothbrush from the holder.

I brushed my teeth in utter silence, but I could still feel him watching me in the mirror. He stood next to me, grabbing his toothbrush as well. My eyes avoided him. If I didn't look at him, perhaps I would be spared.

No.

It was Nathan. Not Adam. Not my dad, Steve. Not Cheryl.

Nathan.

I was still trapped, weighed down by my nightmare. I thought I heard him calling my name, but it was almost like it was through the water that had crashed around me, drowning everything out.

I was lost, I didn't know what to do, how to act. I needed to leave. Get out.

*Get out!*

*Get out! I want you out of my house.*

"Lila!" Nathan yelled. His hand slammed on the wall in front of me, blocking my exit.

I flinched and backed away. My eyes grew wide as I stared at him before I looked down at the ground. With slow, measured steps I walked backward until I hit the wall, my eyes glued to the floor.

"Lila?" he questioned. It was obvious he was taken aback by my actions.

The concern in his voice at my reaction filled my ears. I tried to push it back down, back into its hole, but the dream was still so raw and fresh, reverting me back over ten years. I felt my stomach coiling again.

In my peripheral vision I saw his shadow move against the tile floor. It wavered as he took a step forward. My blood ran cold, my eyes wide, my breathing stopped.

I was frozen in fear.

"Lila?"

I still couldn't respond.

*How could he ever love you? How could anyone?*

I saw his arm rising toward me and I braced myself, trying not to flinch, unsure of what to expect. His fingers moved under my chin and lifted my head up to meet his gaze, but I locked it in place.

He growled and the sound sent a shockwave through me, igniting the spark. His fingers made a light trail around my neck and into my hair, leaving fire in their wake. He wrapped his fingers around my locks and gave a forcible tug. My eyes rose to meet his steel, pained ones.

He paused, staring at me, waiting for recognition to take hold. For me to see that is was him, Nathan, standing in front of me, and no one else. My vision cleared, the pounding in my ears lessening.

My body bowed to his, my chest rising, as if he was pulling me to him with an invisible cord. I knew his touch, *loved* his touch.

I was reminded that I wasn't afraid of his hands on me. Not his. They were aggressive and forceful, but different as night and day to the touch I'd once known. I didn't shy away from Nathan, but moved toward him. My whole body gravitated to his.

The fear melted away when he pressed his body to mine. My heart sped up at his proximity, as it always did; it drummed loudly, drowning out any other sound.

His eyes were dark now; they always darkened when he knew he had me.

Lips came down and pressed hard against mine, his tongue begging for entrance. The moment I surrendered to him, his control slipped; he pushed me into the wall, deepening the kiss, building it into a frenzy.

After a moment he pulled back. His hand released my hair and brushed a few strands away from my face.

"Tell me," he said.

My eyes were frantic as they looked around, waiting for one of the voices to say something.

Nathan's hand grabbed hold of my jaw to keep me facing him. "It's just you and me. Now, tell me."

"A dream," I whispered. "It was just a nightmare, that's all."

He heaved a sigh and stepped away. The small motion tore at my chest, and I found my hand reaching out to him, my eyes wide with fear. I watched sadness and anger cross his face at my reaction.

"Come on," he said, turning and walking to the shower. He leaned in to turn on the water, his back facing me. My eyes wandered over his skin, studying the scars there.

Of their own accord, my feet moved to stand behind him, my hand reaching out and tracing along the lines. He jumped, startled by my approach. As the water heated, he allowed my exploring to continue.

Nathan had scars on the outside to match the scars he held on the inside, where as mine were all inside. The physical pain he endured topped with the emotional...I understood why he said those things, but it still hurt so much to know he wanted to be dead.

I wasn't going to be enough to keep him here. I could barely keep myself standing; how could I save him?

The thought was crushing. I wrapped my arms around his waist and pulled him back to me. I began crying into the space between his shoulder blades, my arms locking in place, keeping him from turning around.

"Lila." His hands pried mine off and he pulled me in front of him.

He gazed down at me, and I knew he could see the tears sliding down my cheeks. He sighed before walking me backward into the shower. The water was hot against my cool skin as we entered the dual spray. I let the water run down my face, into my hair, rinsing away the dream, but my body wouldn't relax.

My eyes traveled over his body as I washed my skin. I scrubbed harder, trying to get the words, the memories off me. After I was rinsed clean, I stepped in front of him and my fingers began trailing along the large scar that ran down the side of his ribs and across his hip.

It was a daily reminder to him each time he looked in the mirror. He couldn't escape his past.

My past might have dictated the type of person I was, but I had control over the person I would become. They couldn't control me anymore. I hadn't seen nor talked to them in years.

It was what I told myself over and over, but there were still times it wasn't enough.

Right then was one of those times.

My fingers returned to tracing the slightly raised, lighter colored skin. I could feel his eyes on me, watching. I looked up to find that his normal cockiness wasn't showing, just pain, confusion, and...*wonderment*?

His fingers trembled as they ghosted over my skin, his lips brushing against mine.

There was only the sound of rushing water, and the hitch of his breath.

Each pass, caress, was like a shock, sending warmth through me to beat back the cold from my dream. Each stroke was bringing me back to him.

My eyes were heavy as they followed his every movement. He took my right hand, and floated it up to his lips. His mouth washed over each knuckle, his eyes on mine the entire time.

His actions held me breathless and spellbound, and spoke volumes in their silence.

He was devoted to me, even if he could never allow himself to love me or say the words; he *did* care. I *meant* something to him.

Tears welled at the corners of my eyes, and I hiccupped as I tried to hold in the emotions trying to burst out of my heart.

He didn't speak, but he didn't need to. Ghosts of my past were trying their damnedest to take me down, while Nathan was pulling me back.

It seemed like he had to be as close as possible, to make me concentrate on him – to focus on what mattered. I felt his beating heart, his breath across my skin. He rained worshipping kisses across my cheeks, down my neck, and along my shoulders. I couldn't ignore the language that his body spoke, it was louder than any verbal sentiment he could ever give. That was all I knew in that moment—he was my anchor.

Once he realized I was over the worst of it, his touches became more urgent, his kisses more intense.

He ran his nose up my neck to my ear. "Relax, baby," he whispered. "Do I have your attention now? I need you here with me." He knew and understood what I needed more than anyone ever had before.

I nodded at his words, and willed my muscles to uncoil, my body relaxing back into him. He was playing my body in a way only he could. No other man would ever be able to make me feel that way.

His fingers slipped into me, while his other hand moved across my chest to tease my nipple. "Come back to me, baby. Don't let them take you from me."

Nathan would not be ignored, least of all because of my past. I loved him for doing that for me. No therapy could ever get me out of my head like that…but Nathan could. He knew what I needed, since his head was equally as fucked up and rife with past trauma.

My legs shook as his fingers pushed deeper, my whole body tensing as I moved closer and closer to the edge. He was pulling me into that trance-like state I craved and needed.

I moaned and pushed my hips back into his as I fisted his hair. "You are *my* cock slut, *my* sex goddess, and *my* beautiful girl. That's all you need to know."

I was panting, so close to release. Every time he called me his, I almost came and sobbed at the same time. I was undone. I couldn't think at all about anything but his possession. My walls clenched around his fingers, my muscles seizing in ecstasy as he pushed me over the edge.

My body was limp against his, my arms at my sides. The spray of the water was cooling my now heated skin.

His hands ran soothing circles on my skin. "Feel better? Are you okay now?"

I nodded as best I could, unable to talk. I soaked up the feeling of him pressed against my back, and tried my hardest to push back the dark doubts that were writhing at the back of my mind.

# CHAPTER 16

It was a long emotional weekend with Nathan, and I was
happy to have my weekly schedule of work ahead of me
to focus on. Work helped to take my brain off my Nathan-
obsession for a little while. At least until I was sucking on a pen.
That move had gotten me into quite a bit of trouble on more than
one occasion. It wasn't entirely intended, but just as he clicked
on pens to think, I sucked on them.

Nathan worked *very* hard that weekend to make sure I couldn't
remember my name let alone walk by the time he was done. He
had returned me to normal, my nightmare pushed to the back of my
mind, and by Sunday night I was back in control of myself. I hated
showing how weak I was to anyone, let alone him. That was why
I created an alternate version of myself. I yearned to one day be as
strong as the woman I made people believe I was on the outside.

I also learned I had given Nathan great power over me. He had the ability to heal me or destroy me, and I didn't know which way it would go. A thought that scared me, but I pushed it back with all the other bad thoughts.

It was a little before seven in the morning when the elevator landed on the first floor, and I stepped into the parking lot, heading to work. After rounding the corner, I stopped in my tracks when I noticed a very familiar man leaning on my car.

I took a deep breath as I walked toward him, unsure why he was waiting for me. I was still pissed about Friday night somewhere in my head, but I felt like Nathan had fucked that loose as well.

Andrew greeted me when I was within earshot. "Hi."

I crossed my arms over my chest. "Hi."

"I came by to apologize." He shoved his hands into his pockets, and I knew he meant it. He always did that when he felt bad about something.

"You did, did you?" I wasn't planning on letting him off the hook, yet. His words hurt, and I wanted to know what sparked them.

"Yes. I thought about the other night and realized what the problem was."

"And?"

He rubbed the back of his neck and let out a nervous little laugh. "I'm jealous. I'm a jealous asshole."

My mouth dropped open, and my breath escaped in a hiss. His confession took me completely off guard and my eyebrows scrunched together. "*What*?"

"My behavior was horrible. I guess I was in shock and, to be honest, a little turned on by the thought of sex with you in a public place. I mean, if you wanted sex, why didn't you come to me? We were always very good in that department. It wasn't just that, though."

"What was it then?"

He gave me a pained smile and sighed. "I can see you've changed since I last saw you. It's not much yet, but there's a light every now and again in your eyes and it wasn't me who put it there. I faced that hard truth the other night. It wasn't your issues that broke us apart, it was me. It was *me* that didn't understand, and I was frustrated with myself for failing. I am never going to be what you need. I am never going to heal you. He understands you, doesn't he?"

I nodded, too stunned by his admission to speak.

"Did I help? At least a little?" His eyes were dim with a sadness I'd never seen in him.

I placed my hand on his chest. "You helped me more than you'll ever know."

He pursed his lips and nodded. "But it wasn't enough."

I gave him a small, sad smile.

"I'm sorry, really sorry about the other night. Please don't hold it against me," he begged.

I gave him a stern look before smiling and pulling him in for a hug. "Just don't hurt me like that again, okay?"

"I'm so sorry. You know I was worried and flew off the handle. I mean, I know you're a horny girl, but rather than some random guy, just jump my bones next time, okay?"

I laughed and pulled back, swatting his chest. "He wasn't random."

"Okay, just jump me next time," he said with a bright smile.

"You're going to get me in trouble."

"Why? Is he the possessive type?"

I laughed at his accuracy but stopped when I felt his body stiffen. His face was no longer lighthearted, but hard.

"Andrew?"

My gaze followed his. Nathan had just stepped through the exit and he was glaring at us. My eyes locked with his, and a shiver ran down my spine at the icy look he gave me.

He was angry. Very angry.

"A little early to be flirting, isn't it? Get going, Delilah, we have a meeting this morning, remember?" He called as I watched him walk into the parking lot, his eyes still locked on us.

"I was just leaving, thank you for the reminder, Nathan," I replied.

He got into his car a few spots down and pulled out, gunning it out of the parking lot.

Andrew spoke up, startling me. "I don't like him."

I turned back to him, noticing my hand was still resting on his chest, and that I was leaning into him.

Shit. I was in deep trouble. I had just inadvertently set Nathan off, and I would be punished all day long by the anger that was rolling off him. He didn't like Andrew, and standing like that with him, laughing? What the hell was I thinking?

"*Why* don't you like him?" I was getting tired of their pissing contest. Though it did make me feel good knowing that two good looking men were on the verge of fighting over me. "You don't even know him."

"Do you?"

"A little," I lied. "We've worked together for a few months now."

"He has a reputation with women, and I don't want that to include you."

I quirked my eyebrow at him. "Is that really it? Because I can assure you he doesn't see me that way."

*No, I'm different from them.*

Andrew sighed and looked down at me. "I've also heard some things about him. He has anger management issues. He was thrown out of the courtroom more than once for his outbursts. That's why he isn't in the courtroom anymore."

I sighed in relief. Andrew only seemed to know water-cooler talk, nothing more. I wasn't sure if I was happy about that or sad. I wanted to know more about Nathan, but I wanted it to come *from* Nathan.

"Well, it's getting late, we need to head in," I said, dropping the Nathan subject.

"Sounds good. I'll see you in the office." He leaned down and hugged me. He placed a kiss on my forehead then walked to his car.

I opened the door to my own car and slid inside. We weren't really running late, I was always early, but I didn't want to argue with Andrew because I knew it would end with me giving myself away. I knew about Nathan's anger, I bore witness to it almost daily, but I had never felt threatened by it. It was all self-destructive in nature.

I looked down at my watch: quarter after seven. My hand turned the key, starting the car and heading to meet my fate; my angry war god of sex and whatever punishment he decided to deliver upon me. My body was already heating up at the thought. It was going to be a very long, very frustrating day and I had Andrew to both blame and thank for it.

I knew I was in deep trouble as soon as I pulled into the parking lot at work. Nathan was standing there, leaning against his car.

Waiting.

How odd they were, the feelings I held. They were so different from what I had known. His anger didn't scare me, it electrified me. It stemmed from his desire for me, and I was vibrating in anticipation.

When he punished me, I could feel my whole being open up to him. He filled me with an emotion I couldn't describe, but I knew I wanted more of it. I craved it.

The car slid into the parking spot next to his, and he started walking toward the building. I grabbed my purse and bag and headed in after him.

It wasn't quite seven thirty; most of our coworkers didn't start until eight or nine, so the building wasn't that busy with people yet. There was a sprinkling of people in the lobby; many of them were headed to the coffee shop before heading up to their respective floors.

He was standing at the elevator bay when I caught up. Alone.

As I approached I could feel the mounting tension rolling off him.

"Thorne." I stepped up to wait beside him, facing front.

"Palmer." His voice was even, covering what was just below the surface.

In my peripheral, I could see him looking at me. His expression was impassive, but his body said something completely different.

The elevator car arrived and we stepped on.

Alone. Damn. We were alone, the space stifling, making it hard to breathe. I wanted him already. Then again, I always wanted him.

The second the doors closed he was on me, pinning me to the wall. Hidden from the camera, his lips crushed mine. Hard, controlling, punishing. The way I loved him; the war god of sex. I moaned into his mouth, and I felt his hips flex, pushing his cock into my stomach.

"What the fuck was that?" he asked, pulling away.

I blinked up at him. "What? Andrew came by to apologize for Friday night."

Nathan growled and reached over to press the stop button and the elevator halted in place. "I can't believe he was fucking touching you and you were letting him. You're mine, remember?" He growled, his fingers pushing my skirt up, making their way up inside my thigh, brushing over my panties, and pressing against the thin fabric.

His other hand ripped the flimsy strip of cotton at the side seam before pushing two fingers all the way in my pussy. My body arched toward his, my hands fisting the fabric on his suit. "I'll make sure you don't fucking forget. Don't *ever* touch another man again, do you understand me?"

"Yes," I agreed with shaky breath, dropping my bag and purse to the ground.

I moaned when his fingers picked up their pace, pushing me to the edge. He let out a groan as his hands moved to reach behind me and squeeze my ass while he lifted my body off the ground, pressing me against the elevator wall. My legs instinctively wrapped around his waist, pulling him closer to where I needed him.

He moaned, his body tense and hard. "Fuck! What you do to me…"

I felt his hand between us, freeing his cock before pushing deep inside me in one hard stroke.

"Mine!" He growled into my ear as his hips pushed harder with each thrust. "Always being a teasing cock slut."

It was hard, erratic, and fast. Punishing me for what he perceived to be my wrongdoings against him; taking his anger out on my body.

He was pounding me hard, but when he felt my body unraveling he would change his angle or slow down. He wasn't going to let me come. My face dropped at the realization.

His whole body tensed, hips thrusting forward one last time, spilling inside me. I whimpered at having been so close, but I knew it was part of my punishment. I was going to suffer all day, and he would make it up to me tonight.

"Let's see you hide this," he challenged through his panting breaths. His mouth latched into the flesh just below my ear, sucking on the skin, teeth digging in. When he was done, he pulled at the scarf that was around my neck, concealing his other marks. "Take this off, and don't put it back on. I want to see who owns that pussy all day long."

I shivered and licked my lips. He leaned down and caught my bottom lip between his teeth, pulling it before pressing his lips to mine.

He sat my feet back on the ground and straightened my skirt with a smirk before righting himself. I watched him lean down, pick my ruined panties off the ground then slide them into his pocket. The thought of him carrying them around with him all day did contradicting things to me; it was embarrassing and a turn on at the same time.

I could feel the moisture of his come wanting to slide down my leg, and he had destroyed my panties, my only defense at stopping it. I needed to find a bathroom, and soon.

I did a frantic search for any evidence as to what we had been doing and found my hair to be a bit mussed, but the rest of my attire seemed okay. I threw my hair up into a quick ponytail while he hit the button to send the elevator back on its course.

The elevator bay was empty when we arrived. Most weren't in yet despite the extra time we had spent on the ride up, and I was able to make my getaway to the bathroom. I freshened up and fixed my hair again before I walked to our office with a throbbing pussy.

It was going to be a long day. I hoped if Andrew came around, he wouldn't smell Nathan on me again.

# CHAPTER 17

He left me wanting, just as he'd intended. Left to sit all day, bare under my skirt, ruined, confiscated panties, and so turned on my thighs were going to be chafed from rubbing together. I was also afraid of a wet spot appearing on my skirt, telling all what a wanton slut I was, though they didn't know who for.

I went about my work, and of course, before ten hit, the Boob-Squad was making their appearance. Two days without seeing him appeared to be torturous.

It would be…for me. Then again, he was with me and not them.

He called me *his*, and was very adamant about that fact, but in terms of a relationship? I wasn't sure. Our constant limbo had me on edge; the only thing that calmed me was his touch. He anchored me then, cementing me to him.

I was happy Kelly didn't stay too long. She was becoming almost scary in her stalker tendencies as she backward stepped out of the office so she was able to continue staring at him for as long as possible. Never mind that she bumped into the coat rack, knocked it over, and sent it crashing into the hall, hitting an intern carrying a stack of files. Paper flew through the air, landing all over the hall and surrounding cubes.

What did she do then? She batted her eyes and tried to help, bending over in a seductive pose, instead of apologizing to the poor intern she accosted. Her actions ruined his day as he now had to reorganize everything.

Thanks to her, the poor intern was going to be in trouble. I remembered being an intern, and some of the lawyers weren't always the friendliest, even more so when something wasn't right.

After almost an hour, I was rocking in my seat; the growing need for some sort of revenge began to grow inside me. Grabbing my phone, I walked to the bathroom and sighed in relief that it was empty. I reached behind me and pulled the zipper down on the back of my knee length, dark grey pencil skirt. I turned down one of the flaps and pointed my phone toward the mirror and snapped a picture.

It was a perfect capture of the top of my ass cheek: round, creamy, and soft. The smooth expanse of skin accentuated the fact I was bare under the thin fabric. Because of him. For him. My hope was that it would put him in the same state I was in.

I surveyed the photo and hit send.

After freshening up, I returned to our office and sat at my desk in a vain hope I could concentrate on my work.

It was soon apparent Nathan wasn't going to allow that.

166

My phone buzzed, I opened the message and froze.

Oh. Fuck.

In front of me was a picture of Nathan's perfect cock: hard, long, and weeping.

*Is this what you want?*

Moisture gathered at the apex of my thighs, and the ache intensified. Knowing he was in that state, mere feet away, and hard for me, was too much. Oh, how I wanted him, needed him, inside me at that moment.

It was all his fault. Wasn't it my turn to take my anger out on him? I sighed, realizing the outcome of that would be my termination. Having the boss come in while I had Nathan tied to a chair as I rode him, naked and screamed in ecstasy, was not the way I saw my time ending with Holloway and Holloway.

I couldn't take it anymore; I had to relieve the tension. I stood and walked around my desk before the sound of my name halted me in my tracks.

"Delilah," Nathan called. "Your phone is buzzing."

I slowly turned to look at him—his expression was impassive, but his eyes were a dark blue. I sighed before returning to my desk and looked at the new message he had sent.

*Don't you even fucking think about going to play with your pussy so you can get off. The only way you are going to come is because I make you. Understood?*

I nodded my head in an unconscious movement and sat back down. My phone buzzed again.

*Good girl.*

I snorted before replying.

*Since when have we been in some weird Dom/sub relationship?*

I watched him shift in his chair before the soft vibrating alerted me to his response.

*Back to work, Miss Palmer. I'll be sure to make it worth the wait.*

With reluctance, I returned to work, hoping to keep him happy and avoid letting him make the day harder on me.

Then again, I found it wasn't me I had to worry about. Andrew came and sat down on the edge of my desk a few minutes before lunch. Out of the corner of my eye, I could see the obvious displeasure looming on Nathan's beautiful features.

The conversation with Andrew was innocent enough: talk of work, lunch, and the poor intern Kelly put into the dog house.

"Lila, it looks like you've got some dirt on your neck." Andrew reached out to brush it away.

A slight twinge of pain alerted me to the "dirt" that he was brushing over. My eyes grew wide, my face heating up. Andrew's hand stilled and he bent down slowly. The motion of his hand faltered before his eyes lifted to meet mine.

"Oh, I see," he said, the realization setting in. His hand dropped away from my skin and he cleared his throat in an effort to disperse the awkward moment. "So, I was thinking that little gyro place for lunch down the street, sound good?"

"Yeah, um, they have really good chicken there," I replied.

I could feel Nathan's gaze, and knew he was looking over at us.

"What?" I heard Andrew question.

I looked up to find them staring at one another. I had the sneaking suspicion that had we been outside the office, they would have been toe-to-toe, trying to duke it out. Whatever "it" was. I was certain it had to be a macho-guy thing. Who had the bigger dick and what-not.

"Nothing, just trying to get some work done in here. Your persistent talking is distracting. Go bother someone else," Nathan replied.

Andrew's jaw tightened and his fist clenched as he stood from his perch on the end of my desk. He faced Nathan, and they continued their silent battle. I let out a sigh that seemed to bring both of their attentions back to me.

Andrew left with a promise to see me at lunch and headed out the door. I turned to look back at Nathan, now glaring at me. He mouthed the word, "Mine," before turning back to his computer and continuing on with his workload.

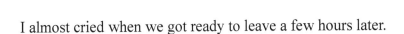

I almost cried when we got ready to leave a few hours later.

Finally.

*Release.*

Nathan and I ended up alone in the elevator for the ride down that night. I was pressed against the wall before the doors even closed. My body bowing into his, my arms around his neck as our lips crashed together, each of us desperate for some sense of control.

He pulled away and pressed his forearms on the wall on either side of my head before continuing our text conversation from earlier. "You would make a great sub." His breath washed over my cheek.

"If the pain of whips and chains excited me," I added. "Do they excite you?"

169

He chuckled. "No, Delilah, they don't, but…" He paused, thinking. "Hmm, tie you up and fuck you any way I want? Oh, yes. I've got some positions I want to try. Ones that would open you up, allowing my cock to slide all the way in. Deep, very deep. You'd like that, wouldn't you? My cock buried all the way inside your tight, little pussy? Fuck, that's what I'm going to do when I get you home."

We hurried back to our building, both of us near bursting from all of our teasing. He at least got off once, while I was left to suffer.

We weren't even through the door of his condo when he had me pinned against the wall, grinding into me. Our movements were frantic and needy as he lifted me up and pulled me back into his bedroom.

He let me go and began loosening his tie, placing it on the bed before removing his suit jacket. His eyes were dark as he looked me over and licked his lips. "Strip for me, baby."

Without hesitation, I began removing my clothing. He was watching me intently as he stripped himself. He groaned when I turned to unzip my skirt and lowered it to the ground, letting him get a good look at my backside as I bent over.

"Yes." He nodded. "You'd make a great sub. Train you up a bit and you'd make a Dom very happy."

I turned and gaped at him.

"What? It's true," he said as he slid his pants off.

I knew he was teasing, trying to get a rise out of me. "I already told you, it doesn't excite me."

He moved to stand in front of me, his hands around my back, pulling me to him. "Have you ever tried?"

"I don't like physical pain that's meant to hurt. And are you telling me you're a closet Dom?"

170

He leaned in to nip my neck. "No, but I do love to dominate, take what I want. You especially. You make it so easy, like you're begging for it. I may not have a playroom and toys, but I *will* tell you what to do because I own your body."

I stepped back, my skin heating. It was true; he did own me, more than he knew. "I can't believe we're having this conversation."

"I can. Tell me, Delilah. Say it."

I looked up at him from underneath my eyelashes. I knew what he wanted. "Yours," I whispered as I bit my bottom lip and looked at his chest.

His fingers made their way to my jaw and tilted my head up so we could meet eye-to-eye. "What was *that*?"

"I'm fucking yours!" I growled out in frustration and embarrassment.

"That's right. Mine."

He wasted no time at all in showing me how much he owned me.

"Feel that?" he asked as he stepped toward me.

I cocked my eyebrow at him. "Feel what? What are you talking about?"

He smirked at me and taunted me in a maddening, delicious way. "You don't feel it?"

"I can feel you looking at me like a piece of meat, if that's what you're talking about?" I was growing tired of the distance between us. I stepped closer and he stepped to the side.

"No, you don't. You have to feel it first."

I groaned in frustration. "Forget it. I thought you were going to make today worth my while, not play stupid games with me. I'm sick of this shit!"

I was ready to grab my stuff and head back out the door. B.O.B. was always willing to help me out. Though he probably needed dusting off from the months of non-usage.

"I'm talking about that knot in your stomach. The wetness dripping down your thigh. Your pussy clenching and pulsing, ready, all just from the way I'm looking at you. If you can't feel it, then you're more fucked up than I thought." He stalked toward me with that damn smirk plastered in place.

My anger was expanding with every second that he kept being such a prick. "Of course I feel those things. I've been feeling them all damn day long. So, what's the point? You already know you do that to me."

"That's right, you *do* feel it. That's me owning your pussy and your ass. Don't you forget it. Andrew doesn't do that to you. I know he doesn't. You get wet for me and nobody else." He got so close I thought for sure he would take me, but he kept enough distance to keep the moisture building and threatening to slide down my thighs.

"You're a sick bastard, you know that?" I said.

"I'm a sick bastard because I see what I do to you? I'm not blind. Just because I can smell your arousal, and hear your heart beat fly when I'm this close to you, does not make me sick." He leaned in even closer so I could feel his humid breath on the side of my throat. "It's all about desire, baby. You want me, and I want you to want me. Quit fucking talking to Andrew, and I'll quit making you wait for your release." He slipped away from me.

Was he leaving the room? What the hell was going on?

I almost began panicking. I knew this was more than jealousy and sex. But somehow he always found a way to confuse me right when I thought I had control again.

"Fine. You don't want me, I'll call Andrew. I'm sure he'd more than love to take advantage of the wet conditions you caused." I said it so flippantly I was shocked he believed me.

His head snapped to look at me, eyes blazing in my direction. He didn't say a word, he didn't have to.

He marched back to me, leaning over me, and hissed out quietly, "I don't need whips and chains to make you obey me. If you want me to touch you, then you'll stay the fuck away from that idiot."

Hands were on my hips, squeezing as they pulled me to him. At that moment, I didn't care what he was saying or what he wanted me to do; his hands were on me, and I couldn't think. I could only feel, and it was heaven.

He bit down around my neck, palmed my breasts and ground his hard cock into me. Each time I moaned out, he smiled and his body became more frenzied. I heard him groan out, "Mine," several times, but I wasn't listening. All I could hear was the sound of his panting and the blood rushing, drumming, in my head.

He had me pinned under his weight and acted like he thought I might leave as he strained to keep me positioned under him. That was the furthest thing from my mind. I wasn't going anywhere; I wasn't struggling to get away. I loved every minute of it, and was trying to get more; it felt so good I couldn't stay still. It was more than my body could bear.

It was what I lived for, what I craved. His hands, his mouth, his insatiable cock were doing things to me that were unspeakable, but at the same time were an all-consuming, pleasurable insanity.

His fingers were working at a furious pace while he sucked hard on my nipples, kissing and nipping his way between the two. I was writhing beneath him; my hands fisted in his hair, my pussy begging for release.

I was stranded, staring over the edge into the brilliant white that awaited me, when his hand and mouth disappeared. He left me pinned with my hands above my head, legs spread wide, and trapped beneath his.

I was in shock for a moment and tried to move, but he had me restrained and at his mercy. I wanted to come, I needed to. The pain and ache was unbearable.

"Please!" I begged.

So close, I had been so close. He knew it and had pulled me back.

"You have no idea how badly I want to slam into you and fuck you until you can't walk. But I like this game and want to keep playing." He breathed hot and heavy into my ear. "You writhing, going insane with the need to come. Should I let you come?"

I didn't answer. He wouldn't dare keep me from coming. Earlier, he had said it would happen and he hadn't let me down thus far.

He started rubbing the length of his shaft up and down my pussy. Each time he hit my clit, I mewled in anticipation of him giving me my release.

"That's it, baby. You like that? Call out my name next time and maybe I'll let you finish," he taunted. He rubbed his dick up my folds and bit into my shoulder; I screamed out his name. I was right *there*. It was infuriating.

Tears were welling up in my eyes, my body burning. He continued to push me further, harder, before pulling away.

"Please!" I wailed. My head shook from side to side, my sanity slipping.

Mine wasn't the only sanity that was slipping, because he moved his legs, freeing my own, before he slammed into me.

I cried out as he filled me and put me on the edge again with one thrust of his hips. There was no pause, no waiting. He pulled out and slammed back in with the same intensity. Over and over.

Out, in. Once more and I was gone, freefalling as I pulsed and clenched around his cock. He howled out, almost like he was in pain when he exploded, unable to hold back any longer.

"Fuck," he whimpered into my neck, and collapsed onto me.

After a moment of rest, he rolled onto his back, pulling me with him. My head landed on his chest, hand over his heart. It was beating beneath my palm at a furious tempo, matching my own. I couldn't move even if I'd wanted too.

His fingers ran through my hair, pushing the damp strands back and over my shoulder. He began humming as he caressed up and down my arm, his lips pressing a light kiss to my forehead as I drifted off to sleep.

# CHAPTER 18

It was two weeks later, on a Monday, and just like all previous Monday's, the Boob-Squad, or the "Nathan Thorne Fan Club," had to make their presence known as soon as they walked in the door. It had been a boobs-on-parade show all day long, and I was ready to explode.

Just before three, the President made her grand entrance. I watched her through the door, as she perked her breasts in her bra before walking in, and I wondered idly if she knew I could see her, or if she just didn't care. Then again, it could be I was invisible to her since Nathan's arrival. I'd officially become another piece of furniture.

Jennifer sat on the edge of his desk. "Nathan, can you take a look at this, please? I think I need to switch something around, but I'm not sure."

She leaned over, pointing to the sentence in question, making sure her breasts were spilling out in front of his face. I could swear every day they were showing more and more. He'd been here over three months, and the conservative garb we all wore, had been thrown out the window in favor of street-walker attire, all meant to entice a being that wouldn't be enticed. He couldn't stand them, but was polite to them anyway.

"Hmm, you need to word this part a little different. As it's written, you've left them an out," he said.

Her head tilted in confusion. "An out?"

I couldn't help but let out a laugh.

They both turned to look at me, and I couldn't stop the laughter. I wasn't sure if the hilarity I found in the situation was due to her stupidity, or if my plan of straddling him with her watching was becoming too close to reality, and I was going insane with desire. He'd been teasing me again all day long, and I was more than ready to jump him as soon as the moment presented itself.

"Sorry," I said, my laughter dying down. "I…umm…just got an email and…it was funny."

Jennifer huffed and roll her eyes. "Shouldn't you be working instead of playing, Delilah?"

I turned to look at her and wondered where my stapler was in the paper tray that was my desk. Would it be bad if I chucked it at her?

Instead, I gave her a sweet smile and stood, grabbing my coffee cup. "Well, you know, emails from Jack Holloway that have bad spellings in them tend to tickle me."

I walked out of the room, but didn't miss Jennifer's jab at me as I went. "God, she is such a bitch. I don't know how you stand being near her."

Nathan chuckled. "It's not easy, trust me."

I wandered down the hall in a Nathan-induced haze, combined with a red haze of the Boob-Squad murder plots that were roaming around in my brain.

In the break room, the coffee was out, again. I started a new pot, and as I waited for it to brew, slammed my head against the cabinet.

"Ah, there's a 'member' in your office," Caroline called from the doorway.

"Ha, what gave me away?"

"The slow destruction of the cabinet with your head?"

I turned to face her, pulling off a small smile. She returned it before her eyes widened and her hand brushed the hair away from my neck.

"What the hell is that?"

*Fuck!*

Nathan decided I was no longer allowed to hide my neck through scarves, and I'd been able to accomplish it with a combination of higher collars and having my hair down. I didn't have one of my normal high-collared shirts on that day due to a heat wave. I just couldn't take it.

In a nervous motion, I pulled my hair back around to try and hide the newest bite mark created by Nathan. It wasn't that I was ashamed, because I wanted to display them, but it wasn't appropriate for work. Especially in our profession.

"Nothing," I replied.

"Nothing my ass, Lila. That is a fucking bruise in the shape of teeth!"

I shushed her, covering her mouth with my hand.

She laughed as I pulled my hand away, and I couldn't help but join.

"Your guy really goes at it, huh?"

"Yeah, he gets a little…overzealous sometimes."

"Am I ever going to meet Mr. Biter? You've been together for what? Over two months now?" Her eyebrow quirked, her expression demanding an answer.

"It's complicated," I explained with a sigh.

"Well?" She motioned with her hand for me to explain.

I looked from side to side, right in time to catch Mark entering.

"Later, okay?"

I returned my attention to the coffee pot and poured myself a fresh cup. Caroline saddled up next to me as we waited for Mark to leave.

As soon as he was out of earshot she was on me again, unrelenting. "What the hell is the big secret, Delilah?"

It was never a good thing when she used my full name. I took a deep breath and let it out slowly.

"Dinner?"

She studied me, her bitch brow quirked. "Fine. But no more bullshit, that's all you've been feeding me for weeks. I want to know everything. *Everything*. Hear me, missy?"

I nodded in agreement. "You better bring some wine."

"Oh shit, it's *that* kind of talk?"

I thought about it for a moment before changing my suggestion to something stronger. "Maybe some tequila."

Caroline wrapped me into a hug and leaned in to whisper in my ear. "Fuck. Who the hell are you messed up with? I can see you're in deep, and that worries me. Because you know I'll fuck him up if he hurts you, right?"

I gave her a hug in thanks before agreeing. I headed back to my office with a fresh cup, thankful that I'd met her. Caroline was such a great friend, and one of the few I'd divulged my past to. It was strange and so wonderful to have someone who cared so much about me.

My hopes were high that Jennifer was gone, but alas she was still there.

Twenty-five excruciating minutes later, she left, and I was free to turn and glare at Nathan. He smirked at me and chuckled at my obvious disdain. All I could think the entire time she was there was, how in the hell did she make it through law school let alone pass the Bar?

The realization she was *acting* stupid popped into my head, and I wanted to slam my hand on the desk at the hilarity. She was stupid, just not law-stupid. She really thought he'd be interested in her if she acted like a dumb blonde?

An email showed up from Caroline, pulling me from my inner thoughts and reminding me to warn Nathan not to come over. I pulled my phone out of my purse and typed up a quick message, and sent it off to him.

*Change of plans. Caroline is coming over. I can't hide you from her any longer. I trust her. I'll come over once she leaves.*

In my peripheral, I could see him looking down toward his hip where his phone rested. His features scrunched up before returning to the computer screen in front of him.

The afternoon wore on, and at about half-past-five Nathan said goodnight, and I decided it was time to call it a day. I gathered up my belongings and walked down the hall to Caroline's office. We headed down to the parking lot, talking about our day before separating and driving to my place.

As soon as we walked in, Caroline headed to the bathroom, and I walked into my bedroom, stripping off my skirt suit and finding some shorts and a tank top to slip on, as well as a set for Caroline.

I was surprised when not five minutes after we had arrived, my front door opened.

What surprised me even more was when I shuffled out of the bedroom, and found Nathan setting down a few bags on my kitchen counter.

He greeted me with a smile. "Hey. I picked us up some food to make dinner with. I was thinking that chicken bake you made a couple of weeks ago. God, that was good."

My eyes were wide as I looked back to the bathroom door, willing Caroline to stay in until I could *shoo* him out.

"What are you doing here?" I asked, shocked he would still come over.

Didn't he get my text? I needed to get him out before Caroline found him.

He smirked and pulled me into his arms as soon as I was within grabbing distance. His mouth moved down my jaw to my neck, nipping and sucking as he went.

"Mmm, well a song on the radio said something about disrobing, then probing. I was thinking we could do a lot of that tonight." His fingers made their way under my shirt to my nipple, tweaking it.

"Fuck," I cried out.

In a sudden movement, he picked me up by my ass and sat me down on the counter, pushing his way between my thighs. Not that I minded, it was my favorite place for him to be, but he was sidetracking me from my mission.

His hand had made its way up my shorts and his fingers began teasing my clit and folds. "You like that, don't you, my little whore?"

My eyes fluttered close. "I love your fucking dirty mouth."

"Mmm, I love it when you say fucking. I like being in control, fucking you how I want. You're so willing to please me, and I love watching you come. No one is as beautiful and sexy as you when you're coming undone around me." His fingers pushed forward with each word.

I stifled a cry, not wanting to alert Caroline and have her come out before I could get Nathan to listen to me.

"Nathan, didn't you get my text?"

"You sent me a text? My phone died after lunch."

My blood ran cold. "Crap!" I cried out, trying to calm the situation that was rapidly spiraling out of control.

This was a very difficult task as my body complied to his every request, silent or spoken.

"You taste so fucking good." He thrust his fingers into me with slow, deep strokes, seeming to be lost to his state of lust.

"Nathan, please…wait."

"You've made me wait all day; I'm not waiting any longer. Wearing that skirt to torture me…you little cocktease."

"You don't… *ah!*" I cried out as he pinched my nipple. "Hold on! W-what skirt?"

"The skirt you were wearing the first time I fucked you in our office." His tongue swirled around the mark on my neck, his teeth nipping at it, his hips grinding his hand further into me.

"Nathan, don't be mad," I said, the sound of the bathroom door closing hitting my ears, making my panic rise.

His hands and lips stopped, his body frozen. "Lila, is there someone here?"

"I tried to tell you…the text I sent."

"Shit." He growled, his grip tightening, his head buried into my neck.

"Oh. My. God!" Caroline's voice rang from the hallway.

I lifted my head to glance over Nathan's shoulder and saw her shocked face. The sound of her purse hitting the tile floor rang out, echoing off the walls.

"Fuck," Nathan whispered into my ear followed by a sigh of resignation.

He turned to look at her, his fingers still buried in my now soaking wet pussy. He removed his fingers, my body letting out a shudder as he did, and brought the fingers to his mouth as he stared at me. Sucking them between his lips, he cleaned his fingers off and returned his attention back to Caroline, who was staring slack-jawed at him.

"Hi, Caroline. Dinner?" Nathan asked, walking to the sink and washing his hands. He moved to the abandoned groceries and began putting them away in their proper place.

Caroline watched on, in stunned silence, while my attention volleyed between the two. I was wondering when she was going to snap out of it, and when I was going to have to explain what was going on.

In the meantime, Nathan moved about my kitchen in fluid motions, putting the groceries away before pulling out the cutting board, and a mixing bowl.

Boy, did I hope I had some sort of drink hidden in my fridge that would help me make it through the night, because I was going to need it and so was Caroline.

The situation was not how I had envisioned revealing Nathan to Caroline. A quiet, wine-filled evening as I slowly divulged the real identity of "Christopher" and explained what I could without exposing too much, too many of his secrets and pains.

Due to bad luck and dead cellphone batteries, I was sitting on my kitchen counter after having been fingered, watching him move around my kitchen with Caroline still staring in shock.

No, not how I saw the evening going at all. I was scrambling, wondering how to tell my best friend I'd been in a fucked-up relationship with my work partner, against company policy, before she exploded.

# CHAPTER 19

The scene in the kitchen was stagnant, waiting to unfold when Caroline finally found her voice. She turned and gaped at me, her mouth popping open and closed, reminding me of a fish. The sight would have made me laugh if the situation hadn't been so serious.

With a deep sigh, I jumped down from the counter and walked to stand in front of her.

"Nathan?" Her voice was almost shrill.

I nodded and turned to find him already cleaning the chicken for me, letting me deal with my friend's initial outburst.

Caroline struggled to string her words together. "How... I mean... Really?"

Again, I nodded.

"But...it's *Nathan Thorne*. You *despise* him." She grabbed my arm and pulled me closer. "*He's* your Christopher?"

"Yes," I replied. "I wanted to tell you, I did…I wanted… "

Caroline silenced me, placing her hand up between us as she stared at Nathan's back. Her fist grabbed the front of my shirt and she dragged me into the living room. Her eyes were still glued on the kitchen when she stopped and pulled me closer, her face mere inches from mine.

"Let me get this straight. You are fucking Nathan-fucking-Thorne?" she hissed.

I swallowed hard before responding. "Yes. Caroline, I…"

"Shush." She slapped her hand over my mouth. I stared at her in shock. "*You* are fucking Nathan Thorne?"

I rolled my eyes and nodded. How many times did I have to tell her?

"Holy. Fucking. Shit. You are fucking Nathan Thorne." She smiled, beaming at me.

I grabbed her hand and removed it from my mouth. "I wanted to tell you. It's just…well… What are you smiling about?"

Her grin widened. "*You*, Lila Palmer, are fucking *Nathan Thorne*."

"Yes, Jesus, how many times do you have to say it?"

"That means the Boob-Squad doesn't have their hands on him. That means that *you* gave him all the hickies I've seen on him…and he gave you yours." Her mouth popped open. "That means the reason he hasn't gone to the bar in the last few months is because he's been with you."

"Yes. I couldn't tell you because…well…what we have is complicated."

Caroline nodded in understanding. "Yeah, you said 'Christopher' was broken. Jesus…Nathan doesn't seem to be like that. I don't see it."

186

"He has a better act than I do."

Caroline stood there, her arms folded across her chest, a contemplative look etched on her face. A moment later, she made an abrupt turn and walked back into the kitchen. I followed, wondering what was going on.

Thus far, I found his response more disturbing than Caroline's. I had no idea what was going on inside his head. As soon as he saw Caroline, he began the mindless task of putting groceries away and prepping for dinner.

I watched on with a wary eye as Caroline approached Nathan's back. He turned at the sound of her footsteps against the tile. She stopped about a foot in front of him, invading his personal space. His act was perfectly in place, and he seemed as cool as ever.

"*You.*" She pointed her finger at him, in an accusing way. "Hurt her and I'll fuck you up. Understood?"

I let out a little giggle from the expression that formed on his face; his eyes were wide in fear of the woman in front of him. She was over half a foot shorter than him, and about half his weight, yet she was standing there intimidating a former federal prosecutor.

"Understood."

"Are you being safe with my girl? I've seen you with some floozies."

"I'm clean. Promise."

"Better fucking be, bucko."

And with that, she was smiling again.

Warmth spread in my heart, the love for my friend growing. This was something new, something I had never experienced but had read about and seen in movies. The best friend warning the guy. Caroline was already friends with both Andrew and I when our relationship began, so I had missed this experience then.

"So, you two…" Caroline began, diving in, now that her brain was working again. "When did all of this start up? Did it happen one day here, or was it an office tryst one night type of thing?" Caroline smiled and waggled her eyebrows.

I could feel the blood flooding to my face, and my eyes widened. Nathan froze mid slice, clearing his throat before continuing.

Her expression returned to the one of shock that had frozen on her face before "Seriously? In the office? In *your* office?"

I nodded, swallowing hard, too embarrassed to speak.

"Wow, you're my kinky idol now, Lila." She leaned back against the counter with a smile.

"What? I…he…" I stammered in protest.

"I bet it was hot."

"Of course it was hot," Nathan answered, turning to look at Caroline, and speaking freely for the first time. "Look at her. She is fucking gorgeous and sexy as hell. Sin should be her middle name."

Caroline stared as he spoke, the grin spreading on her face. "So, have words of love been shared?"

At the mention of love between us, Nathan stopped what he was doing. My eyes were glued to his back, watching the muscles in his shoulders and back tense.

"What did I say?" Caroline asked, her head moving between the two of us, startled by his sudden shift.

I was used to his mood swings, but Caroline was used to the mask. He turned from his spot against the counter and his eyes found mine, holding my stare for a moment before he moved to the sink and washed his hands.

"I think it's about time you took over. I'm going to go change," he declared as he dried his hands.

"All right. Thank you." I hated that his mood had soured.

As he walked past me, he stopped and leaned down, placing a quick kiss to the top of my head, surprising me, before heading up to his condo.

Caroline stared after him. "What the hell was that?"

I let out a sigh as I headed to the sink and washed my hands before moving to finish cutting the chicken Nathan had started. I tried to explain to her as best I could. "Nathan is…complicated… and damaged. What you see on the outside, at the office, is just a façade. Like pretty new siding over an old dilapidated house."

Caroline considered this for a moment, mulling over everything. "But, you consider yourselves boyfriend and girlfriend, right? Dating?"

I bit my lip, trying to find the best way to describe our status, or lack thereof. "No, our relationship is…undefined. The only word we use is 'mine.'"

"Well…it may not be a declaration of a relationship, but it is a claim, I suppose. You only see each other?"

"Yes. Every day, actually."

"Every day? Do you sleep in the same bed?"

"Yes."

"Every night?"

"Yes." My hand slowed down as I continued to cut into the food, realizing just how pathetic it all must sound to her.

"Wow…just…I don't know, Lila. I see now why your insomnia has gone away if you're sleeping with him every night." Her brow scrunched in concern. I could see the sadness in her eyes. "This is not what I was expecting you to tell me tonight."

"I didn't want to keep it from you, but the way things happened between us was unconventional."

"So, that night at the bar, that was after the office romp?" she asked, and I nodded. "I wondered why he was acting so weird. He didn't like Andrew near his girl."

I rolled my eyes. "He doesn't like Andrew at all, and the feeling is mutual. I don't get it."

"Men. I know you don't understand them – who does? – but, let's put it this way…you used to be Andrew's and now your Nathan's. I *know* Andrew still has a thing for you and Nathan clearly does. Neither of them likes the thought of you with the other."

Her inquisition was hitting so many nerves, I had to concentrate on cutting, otherwise I was going to lose a finger. I squinted, trying to focus on every little movement I made. "But Andrew doesn't know about us."

"Doesn't matter. He's a guy and therefore all other guys are possibilities of taking you. Something Nathan seems to do very well." She said with a wink.

I felt the blush creep over my skin. "Yes, he does."

"I wonder what happened to him."

I shrugged my shoulders. "All I know is he used to be a federal prosecutor and that something bad happened, scaring him."

"Oh, I know. We can Google him!"

She bounced with excitement and ran to her purse. As soon as she had her phone in her hand, she began searching for him. My hand reached out and covered the screen, causing her gaze to snap up to mine, confusion swirling in her eyes.

I stared at her. "You can do that, but don't tell me. I tried once, but when the search came up I closed it. I want to hear it from him when he's ready." Caroline studied me for a few moments, and all I could do was blink back at her. "What?"

"Oh my God, you're in love with him."

"Is that what this feeling is?" I asked, reflecting on all the emotions that swirled around inside me.

My hand rested on my chest, right over my heart. Love? Could it really be? I'd never been in love before, not even with Andrew...in fact, the only love I had was my platonic love for Caroline and my foster family. The idea both thrilled and frightened me.

She smiled at me, her hand moving to brush a strand of hair behind my ear. "Yes, sweetie, that's what that feeling is."

After that, her attention was drawn back to the shiny piece of technology in her hand. I watched Caroline as she surfed for Nathan, looking for the information to quench her curiosity. I knew the moment she found what she was looking for. Her expression said it all.

As I feared, her smile of excitement fell from her face, sadness replacing it. Her hand moved to cover her mouth, her body sagging against the counter for support.

Her body language answered all my unspoken questions. Again, I felt the pang in my chest. Would I be enough to keep him with me?

I heard the sound of a key in the lock followed by the door closing; Nathan had returned.

"How's dinner coming?" he asked, and I couldn't help but lick my lips at the sight of him when he rounded the corner.

Nathan was sin in a suit and equally as sinful in jeans and a t-shirt. To be honest, anything or nothing on Nathan, it didn't matter, he always looked delicious.

Caroline walked up to stand a few feet right in front of him. "I'm sorry. I Googled you. Don't worry; I won't say anything to anyone, even Lila. She wants to hear it from you when you're ready," Caroline blurted, speaking fast, and wide-eyed.

Nathan's eyes rounded in what looked like fear and he swallowed hard. He leaned down toward her and lowered his tone. "I need to request that you please make sure you do. Only a few trusted people in the office know. I stress this because what you learned isn't the whole story, nor wholly true, and I don't want rumors spreading."

"I promise. I won't say a word. It's not my place anyway," she assured him.

Her reaction flared my curiosity again. In one search he'd gained her trust and devotion, a hard feat.

"Thank you, Caroline."

The rest of dinner went off without a hitch. There was no more talk about Nathan's past, and only a few times did Caroline bring up Andrew's name. She did it just to watch Nathan's reaction to it, of that I was certain. Her eyes lit up every time, and she smiled when his eyes narrowed. She'd then look to me with a knowing smile. We talked about work, the office, and Nathan's fan club.

It was then that Nathan found out what I called his admirers; I'd never ever told him. He also vowed he would forever refer to them as "B.S." so that we could be discreet when talking about them in the office. He also assured Caroline that he didn't buy any of the B.S.'s BS.

When he laughed at his little joke, I couldn't help but stare in wonder at the smile that formed. It was new. It wasn't forced, nor a small one. I'd never seen him smile like that, and I was awestruck at the beauty of it, and the light feeling coming off Nathan at that moment. I etched it into my memory; there was a chance I would never see him like that again.

Around nine, Caroline said her goodnights and that she'd see us in the morning, promising to act normal.

I turned to him as we cleaned up the mess from dinner. "Did your phone really die?" I had to admit, I loved that we were able to spend time with someone else knowing about us. It was liberating.

He smirked and my suspicion flared up. Had he known and come anyway?

"Yes, it died after lunch."

"How long after lunch?" I asked.

A devilish grin spread across his lips. "Sometime around when you got coffee. I was surprised to find she followed you home. I thought she would come over later."

"Oh, God, you did read it and came over anyway?"

"Technically, I read half of it…then my phone died."

"Unbelievable!"

"I thought it was a good idea. One of your friends should know, in case…" He trailed off. I didn't ask him to elaborate. I'd learned that sometimes it was best to let certain things go. He would tell me in his own time.

"You couldn't have given me a heads up? I was freaking out!"

He placed a kiss on my neck. "I'll make it up to you."

"How?"

He wiggled his eyebrows. "Oh, I think I have a few tricks up my sleeves…and down my pants."

I shook my head and chuckled. "Do you, now? I'm not sure I'm convinced of your professed prowess."

A complete lie. He had shown me again and again his skills in the bedroom – or wall, living room, elevator, shower, just about anywhere and everywhere.

"Are you challenging my ability to make you come and come often?" he questioned in mock incredulity.

He was being playful. Just what had gotten into him that evening, I didn't know. Maybe he had taken his meds when he was upstairs. Whatever it was, I wasn't going to complain. I liked this side of him, a lot.

After the dishes were dry and put away, he leaned over and picked me up, tossing me over his shoulder.

I cried out in protest. "Nathan!"

"Time for bed, Number One."

"Number One?" I questioned.

"Yes, you're number one in the Boob-Squad."

"Says who and why?" My hands reached out to grab his perfect ass, hovering in front of my eyes.

He cried out my name in surprise, smacking my ass before answering. "Because you show me a hell of a lot more of your tits than they do. Way more of them, and way more often."

We reached my bedroom and he dropped me down onto the bed, his body crashing on top of mine. His hands roamed up my arms, moving them, pinning them above my head. The bulge in his pants was being pressed into my hot center, right where I wanted him. My hips tilted upward to grind against him, resulting in a hiss before his hooded eyes came within mere inches of my own. Neither one of us could stop smiling for the next several breaths as he continued to nestle himself between my thighs and rock me a little back and forth.

Then the mood shifted as his eyes darkened.

"Something you want, baby?" His voice was low and husky, and I shivered at his question. I lifted my hips in response, earning another small hiss. "Words, Delilah. Tell me in words what you want."

"Kiss me," I replied, wanting to feel his lips against mine, to taste him.

"Where?"

My breathing picked up, hips rocking.

"Everywhere," I whispered, unable to get any other sound out.

His lips crashed into mine, his tongue sliding in and tasting me.

Sex was where we felt safe; where we knew each other. Nothing else seemed to matter when we took a hold of each other that way. I didn't have to worry about Caroline, about the next day at the office. None of it mattered because I was with him and we both had what we wanted. There was sanity in the chaos. And breath back in my body.

He released my lips, his eyes staring into mine with a softness that had my heart hammering. "I meant it you know."

My eyes fluttered at the soft caress of his fingers moving along my cheek and down my neck. "Meant what?"

"When I told Caroline how beautiful and sexy you are." His lips ghosted across mine before his eyes scrunched in pain and he shook his head. "I don't know how anyone could ever tell you different, but they were wrong. Believe me, baby, they were so wrong about it all. It kills me and pisses me off to no end to know that there are more of their lies rattling around inside that head of yours."

Tears welled in my eyes, and I had to look away. "You can't know they were all lies."

He cupped my cheek, bringing my gaze back up to his. "Yes, I can. I may be fucked up beyond repair, but I can still see the truth. You deserve so much…you deserve a loving heart and a caring hand, understanding and kind words to erase the false ones."

My heart clenched, a tear releasing from my eye and rolling down my cheek. The sincerity in what he said took me by surprise. My arms wrapped around his shoulders, pulling him closer as I buried my face into his neck, a small sob breaking free.

His arms wrapped around me like a secure blanket. He made soothing sounds as his hand brushed over my hair.

"It's okay, Honeybear, I've got you."

I didn't know if he knew the implications of what he said, but I wanted all of it, and I wanted it with him.

# CHAPTER 20

L ater that week, thanks to the Boob-Squad, we became aware of the accused offenders of the alleged affair. Sadie from our accounting department and Will from tax law. They were not only hiding a relationship, but were expecting.

The story running rampant was Benjamin and his wife were at the OB/GYN for a checkup when they bumped into Will and Sadie. Benjamin's wife told one of her friends about it who told another, who told another, and so on, before it ended up in one of the biggest office gossip's ear. You didn't tell Sheila, Mr. Holloway's assistant, anything that you didn't want spread around.

I felt bad for them, worrying about when the situation came to a head. I understood Holloway & Holloway's policy and why it was in place. I was there during the Antonio and Karen blow up. The difference I found here was that Sadie and Will worked in separate departments and never interacted for work, while Karen had been Antonio's legal assistant.

Mr. Holloway could amend it so that they could keep their jobs because they were in different parts of the business. I knew Jack was kind and just trying to protect his business and his employees, but if he couldn't amend it for this couple, I knew there was no hope for Nathan and I. Either way, we would be separated at work, both of us fired for our indiscretion.

I feared that day.

Even though I couldn't express my feelings for him at the office, just having him near soothed me. Thinking about not having him there was enough to almost send me into a panic. I wanted to be near him.

Always.

<hr />

I was amazed how fast time moved since Nathan had come into my life. Two weeks had passed since Caroline had joined in on our little secret. She'd been doing a great job hiding the fact that she knew anything was going on. In fact, she joined in with me against Nathan and the Boob-Squad in our less than friendly, sarcastic banter in the office, and then laughed all through lunch about the reactions.

I think she was having way too much fun, but that's what made it great because Nathan would laugh at night about the things Caroline had said during the day.

Nathan laughing was something I wanted to encourage as much as possible. I couldn't wait to tell him that night that Caroline had called Tiffany a "street-walker-wannabe," due to the outfit she had picked out that day.

I shuffled the groceries, setting them on the floor of the elevator as I stripped off my suit jacket, revealing the tank top beneath. I sighed as the cool air hit my heated skin.

I hated having to hide my arms, but the bruises...I knew people wouldn't understand.

While folding my jacket over my arm, I leaned down to riffle through my purse in search of my keys. I found them just in time for the elevator doors to open and picked everything back up. I twisted the key in the lock and made my way inside, kicking the door closed with my foot.

The sound of voices could be heard as I walked to his kitchen to put the bags down. It didn't sound like the television and one of the voices I was certain was Nathan's.

"Nathan?" I called out.

There was a pause and some more mumbled words before his voice rang out. "In the living room."

I crossed the hall and turned the corner before stopping dead in my tracks.

Nathan had a visitor.

Nathan *never* had visitors.

"Oh, I'm sorry," I apologized, but I wasn't sure what for. Interrupting them? Seeing them? Being me?

I was sure my eyes were wide as I took in the graying brown hair and crisp blue eyes of the attractive older man, occupying a cushion on Nathan's couch. My attention moved back to Nathan and he beckoned me to his side. I was nervous as I walked to stand next to him, still in shock at seeing another person in his home and not knowing how to act because of it.

"Lila, I'd like to introduce you to my father, George Thorne. Dad this is Lila, my...my Lila." His grip tightened on my waist, pulling me closer to him.

A gasp drew my attention back to the man I now knew as Nathan's father. He was looking at me with surprised eyes, filled with joy.

He held out his hand. "Lila, it's a real pleasure to meet you."

Stepping away from Nathan, I walked forward and took his hand in mine. "You as well, Mr. Thorne."

His fingers curled around my hand. "George, please."

His gaze moved down to my arm, and shock covered his entire face. It was quickly replaced with a forced smile.

I looked down to see what brought about the change.

Nathan's hand print on my bicep and the light bruises on my wrist from where I had pulled at his tie when he had restrained me to the bed the previous night.

"Are you staying for dinner, George? I'm making chicken marsala." I pulled my hand free from his and stepped back to Nathan's side.

"No, no thank you, my dear. I would love to, but Mrs. Thorne is expecting me home soon," he said, that forced smile still in place, and his jaw tight.

I could feel the tension in the air as George looked from Nathan and back to me.

"Well...I'll just let you return to your conversation, and I'll go work on dinner. It was very nice meeting you, George."

As soon as I was out of view, I heard George speak in hushed, harsh tones.

"Nathan, are you…hurting her?"

"What?" Nathan sounded truly bewildered.

"Son, she has bruises on her biceps and wrists. Are you abusing that girl?"

I stopped all movement in complete shock. He thought Nathan was hurting me? The thought made me sick. Nathan healed me, he never hurt me. The thought that someone, anyone, let alone his own father, had doubts about the kind of man Nathan was, didn't sit well with me. I couldn't let it continue. I wouldn't.

I stormed out of the kitchen and into the living room, my hands at the hem of my shirt.

"He is not hurting me," I said, my voice raised and shaking. How could he even consider his son capable of abuse?

"Lila, no." Nathan reached for my hands. The panic was evident in his features.

"No. He has to see. I will *not* allow your father to think you are abusing me! That you are *hurting* me!" I argued, pulling at my top.

Nathan's hands pushed mine back down.

"I said no, baby. Only I get to see you without your clothes, even if my father is a doctor."

We stared off, neither backing down from our positions.

"Fine," I conceded, my hands released the hem. Turning to George, I lifted my hair up, exposing the area hidden beneath. He gasped as his gaze took in the obvious bite marks on my neck and shoulder, hand print bruises on my arms, and my tank top exposed the bruises and bites along my chest. "I'm an easy bruiser, Mr. Thorne. Malice and hate does not mark me. Nathan's passion and need do. I know the sting of an angry hand and *that* is something Nathan does not have with me."

Sadness etched George's face and I could see the same emotion in Nathan's. He lifted his hand up and caressed the marks he had left there. Leaning forward he placed light reverent kisses where he'd just touched.

I grabbed a hold of Nathan's shirt and pulled his collar back aside to show his father the matching bite marks I'd given his son. "See? He's not doing anything to me that I don't want him to. We just get a little…carried away, is all."

George cleared his throat, gaining Nathan's attention again. Nathan pulled his head back, his hand gathering mine and lowering it down to our sides.

"I'm sorry, Lila, Nathan. I was just concerned. It's apparent your anger is getting out of control. I mean, look at what you've done to the entryway in the past few months. I was just worried that you…Darren told me you haven't been by in months. He wanted me to let you know he won't refill your prescriptions anymore unless you get back in to see him."

Nathan's hand released mine and moved to his face, rubbing at his eyes. "I know, I know."

"This is serious, son. I want you to get better. I want to see you smiling again. I want to see you happy." George's gaze flickered to me. "But you'll never be any of those if you don't get help."

Nathan snorted in response. "Yeah, because the last three and a half fucking years of therapy have done wonders."

"It only works if you actually want help and work at getting better. Not going in months, not talking to him about your new relationship… Things are changing for you, and you need some support to help you get through this, work through this. To move on, so you aren't weighed down any longer. You deserve it, as

202

does Lila," George said, love and concern written all over his face. "You're going through your meds at a much faster rate than usual. David also told me you missed your last appointment."

"I had to reschedule it, that's all." Nathan's tone was a bit harsh in his agitation. "And I'll call and get in with Darren this week."

"Because you're out of meds?"

Nathan sighed and nodded in agreement, his father seeing the truth.

"Well, I should be headed out now before your mother begins to worry." George pushed off the couch and moved to stand in front of Nathan. He wrapped his arms around his son, pulling him into a fierce hug. "I love you, Nathan."

Nathan hugged his father back with matched ferocity. "I love you too, Dad."

To my surprise and shock, George wrapped his arms around me and whispered in my ear. "Thank you, Lila. Please take good care of him."

I stood frozen in his arms for a moment, and then with slow, tentative movements, my arms wrapped around him. I still wasn't good with hugs, and sudden ones, such as George's, were the hardest.

"Have a good night. I hope to see you at dinner sometime soon. Your mother misses you," he added before turning for the door. "Oh, and don't forget to bring this lovely young lady with you. Your mother would love to meet her. It was such a pleasure meeting you, Lila."

"You too," I said as he stepped through the door.

We stood in the living room for a few minutes before I broke the silence.

"Dinner?"

A grumble from Nathan's stomach caused us both to laugh, breaking through the tension in the room.

"Please."

After dinner, Nathan grabbed my hand and pulled me to him, bringing my lips to his with a gentle touch.

The kiss intensified and a few gropes later, he was pushing me against the counter. He released my lips and trailed kisses and nips down to my ear. "Come on, Honeybear, let's move to the couch. I need a new batch of bruises on my body so I can scare the neighbors…"

I rolled my eyes at the ridiculous nickname he had concocted for me and the silly things he was saying. The name started after the event at the bar with Andrew, when he'd interrupted us. Its use had increased to where it was now being spoken at least once daily. I was sure it was being done to annoy me.

However, I couldn't stop the joy that filled me every time he said it; the warmth that spread through my heart.

Walking into the living room, he sat down on the couch before reaching for the remote.

"Why is it that you don't want me to see Andrew, but your fan club can hang all over you?" I asked as I moved in front of him and straddled his legs before moving lower. His hands moved up to my waist, his thumbs making small circles on my skin. "That sounds like a double standard to me, Mr. Thorne."

"It's simple. I have no interest in any of them and I have never touched, nor will I ever touch, any of them. Andrew, on the other hand, has shared a bed with you, been in a relationship with you, had his cock inside you." He growled the last part, his fingers flexing around my hips. "I know he wants you and you have every opportunity to go back to him. He wants to take what's mine."

"They want what's mine," I pointed out. "And how do you know Andrew wants me?"

Nathan sighed and gave me an exasperated look.

"Delilah, I know you're naïve in some regards, but trust me, he wants you back. I've seen the way he looks at you. And, yes, the girls may want what's yours, but have I ever touched them? Have I ever given any indication I wanted to pursue any of them? I don't want to pursue anyone."

"You pursue me," I said, regretting it as soon as the words passed my lips.

*Bad idea, Lila.* Monumental sized bad idea.

His mood change was swift, and he became sullen, his hands stopping their movement across my skin.

"Yes. Against my better judgment."

"What does your judgment tell you to do?"

"It says that it's better for you if we weren't together, but that line of thinking makes me want to go mad and I find it even harder to let go of you."

"So…you're saying…that your heart pursues me?" I pressed, praying to God he would give me some slight indication of how he felt about me. Even a hint that he cared for me. I *needed* to hear it. I desperately craved the affections of his heart. "Your head rejects me, but your heart wants me?"

After some thought, I realized it would have been better if I'd hit him with a frying pan at that moment, rather than let those words slip past my lips.

His eyes widened as he stared unblinking at me. His grip tightened, pulling me closer, his forehead leaning to rest against mine, his eyes screwed tight. Tension was radiating off him. The turmoil happening inside him was my own selfish doing and was difficult to watch, making me feel helpless. Hadn't I accepted he didn't operate this way, that he might not ever be able to say the words or express any real, lasting affection for me?

"I'm sorry…" I trailed off, my hands creating soothing motions on his back.

He wrapped his arms around my waist and pulled my body flush with his. His lips trailed down my neck and across my shoulder, dropping my tank top strap down my arm, ending the conversation there and moving on to what we both needed.

To the only way he knew how to express his feelings.

# CHAPTER 21

"**O**h, my God. Could you quit flaunting your tits around? I'm getting so sick of looking at yours, I can hardly stand to look at my own. And, by the way, if he hasn't taken the bait yet, he isn't going to." Caroline was attempting to get the point across to two B.S. members, Kelly and Tiffany.

I was having a very difficult time keeping my coffee in my mouth. It was threatening to fly out all over my desk, files and computer screen. There was nothing worse than coffee stained documents.

I chanced a glance over at Nathan, also attempting not to laugh, his hand covering his mouth, concealing his upturned lips. His eyes betrayed him, laugh lines crinkling in the corners.

*Laugh lines.*

My addiction to seeing them was growing stronger every day. Each time he smiled, I wanted more.

Caroline was living up our secret to the fullest by giving it to the Boob-Squad.

"Whatever, Caroline." Kelly sneered, pulling me from my internal musing, before grabbing Tiffany's arm and leaving our office.

We continued to snicker about them after they left, our good mood making the office feel light.

It was short lived when Andrew's voice rang out around the walls.

"Morning!" he greeted with a huge grin.

He and Nathan exchanged a brief glare before he turned back to me and smiled.

Andrew seemed to note our grins. "Did I miss something?"

"Just Caroline showing the Boob-Squad why she rocks," I answered.

"Awesome!" He reached out to Caroline for a high-five. "Oh! Hey, Lila, guess who I ran into last night?" he asked, plopping down on the chair in the corner of our office.

"Who?"

"Teresa," he stated.

My face lit up with a smile. "I thought she and Armando were still in Europe."

"Yeah, apparently Joan found another kid that needed a home and, well, you know Teresa."

I smiled as a picture of Joan Stateman popped into my head. It was with Joan's help that I got out and was able to see what a normal family was like. It was because of them I had gotten as far as I had in life, despite my rocky start. I owed them my life.

"Yeah. She never passed up the opportunity to help any child," I replied with a smile.

"What are you two talking about?" Nathan asked.

Andrew looked to me, I looked to Caroline, Caroline looked to Andrew, and we all looked to Nathan.

"Well, umm, Teresa was my foster mom for a little while."

Nathan's eyes grew wide as he stared at me in shock, his jaw slack.

Caroline jumped up, pulling on Andrew's arm. "Come on, Andrew, let's go get some coffee."

"Umm, okay," he mumbled, looking between Nathan and I in confusion.

Caroline shut the door as they exited. Another reason to love her.

"What?"

I bit my lip and took a deep breath. Only Andrew and Caroline knew what I was about to divulge to Nathan. I wasn't hiding it; I just couldn't stand the twenty million questions people always had that followed. My ex-family's words still haunted me. Why would I want to open that up to everyone?

I let out a long breath before speaking. "A few months before my seventeenth birthday, I contacted a children's law center to be emancipated from my family."

"Jesus fucking Christ." Nathan ran his hand through his hair.

"Joan, she was my lawyer… In fact, she was the one who got me interested in law. Anyway, we never made it to court, child services stepped in. Joan knew of a couple who liked to help out teens in situations such as mine, and so I moved to Indianapolis between my junior and senior year and finished out high school here." My hands twisted in my lap as I went into details of my teenage years that few knew. "Teresa is a sweet loving woman who was very patient with me. She was my first hug."

"Your first *hug*?" I could see the wheels turning in his head.

I nodded. "My first real hug since I went to live with my father. Armando worked with me, showing me that what my father and stepbrother did was not how most men behaved. It took me a long time to trust him. I waited for the insults to slip from his lips, but only words of encouragement and caring ever came from him." A small smile crept onto my lips. "Armando was a bit awkward, but that made him more endearing. Noah was also there, he helped as well."

"Who's Noah?"

"Noah lived with Teresa and Armando when I moved in. He's a year older than me. He had come from a more abusive home than I did. When his dad sent him to the hospital, the law stepped in. He was headed to college that fall; something he never thought he would do. He showed me what a brother was supposed to be like. He was better adjusted than I was to people; he had a better support system."

Nathan's expression morphed before my eyes. So many emotions passed over his face as he digested it all. Every bit of pain, anger, and remorse that crossed his face, solidified what kind of a man Nathan was inside. Especially compared to those I grew up with. The emotions he felt were not directed at me, but *for* me. I could see it in his face; he wanted to hurt those who had hurt me.

"Do you want to know what my favorite Disney movie was?" I asked out of the blue.

He looked up at me with soft eyes, and my heart fluttered. "I want to know anything you want to tell me."

"Cinderella. I used to pretend I was her and a prince would come and take me away." A sad smile tugged on my lips. "It was when I was fourteen and Adam kicked me so hard he broke two ribs that my dream came crumbling down. The hospital, of course, believed the story my father told about what happened. He told them we were rough housing when the truth was Adam was pissed off, and I was an available punching bag. It was then I realized if I wanted out, I had to do it myself; no one was going to come rescue me. There was no prince on a white horse."

When I looked over, Nathan's fists and jaw were clenched tight. "Did he do that to you often?"

"It was mostly verbal. Yeah, he'd push me into walls every day, but a few times a year he would go off, and I'd be in the hospital again. I was 'clumsy' you see. Clumsy Lila hurt herself again. Tripped and fell down the stairs. Can't walk across a flat surface without falling. Clumsy, clumsy Lila."

I sat silent and still for a moment to collect myself; I'd been willing the tears away. When I turned to look at Nathan, he was staring at me with sadness and anger. I wasn't sure how to make it better, so I kept silent.

"Did your father hit you?" he asked through clenched teeth.

My head unconsciously twitched at the thought, and Nathan hissed out a soft "fuck."

"He would slap me, but he never punched. He couldn't stand to look at me, and if his eyes met mine, he would snap."

"Why then?" he asked.

"Because he was staring at his eyes on the face of a woman he slept with once, years before, and he hated her for ruining his life. He hated me."

"Your mother?"

211

"She died in a car accident when I was five. Steve, my father, knew about me, but didn't want anything to do with me. When she died, he was listed as my guardian. I don't think she ever meant for me to go with him, but her own parents were dead, and she had no other family. I'd never met him before that day."

I took a deep, shaky breath. It was always hard to talk about my father, a man who held so much contempt for me. "He was married by then, and his wife had a son of her own. They all hated me for disrupting their family. It was the talk of the town because he was prominent in the community, so he couldn't ditch me once word got out. I wish he had, but they had to think he was the kind of man that did the right thing. So, he took me home and ignored me. He refused to soothe me when I was upset; he would yell and scream instead. He put on his proud father face when out, but when at home, I was left to fend for myself. Child protective services would be all over his ass these days."

Nathan's voice was strained, every muscle in his body tense. "How did you survive?"

I snorted. "He taught me independence through neglect. That was probably his downfall."

His hand reached across the desk to mine. "You did nothing to deserve it. You know that, right?" His thumb was making soothing circles across my fingers.

I knew he wanted to do more, but we couldn't in the office. It would have to wait.

I nodded as best I could. Words would fail me because I couldn't agree, not fully, and then he would see through me.

We returned to our work, Nathan peering over at me from time to time to make sure I was all right, and I knew he could see I wasn't. I felt out of sorts for the remainder of the day; my mind kept wandering back to those awful times in that house. I couldn't even eat lunch, still bombarded with the memories.

The rest of the day was pretty uneventful. It was long, but without drama or encore performances from the Boob-Squad. Which was good. I still couldn't shake the memories and they were dragging me down.

It was several hours later when we returned to my condo. He could sense my sullen mood and wordlessly helped me out of my suit while he stripped out of his own. He made us a simple dinner, because he couldn't cook much, but it was appreciated all the same. I sat on the couch flipping through channels. Once we were done and the dishes were washed, he pulled me into the bedroom and laid me on the bed.

That night, he paid great attention to me, worshipping my body. And like that morning in the shower, he used his touch to bring me back to myself, back to him. It was softer, but still intense, passion flowing from him into me. His presence over-powered everything else. With each thrust, he was pulling on the rope that tied us together, pulling me back to him. His arms were wrapped around my body, holding me to him. When he pushed me over the edge, I felt my heart spring open.

I was home.

We were one in that moment, together again, bound to each other in a way neither of us understood, but were beginning to accept.

I was in love with him. I loved Nathan Thorne.

Everything solidified, and I knew the truth behind those words. I finally found my home, the place where I belonged.

# CHAPTER 22

N athan was always stiff and sore in the mornings; some symptoms showed more than others. That day fell into the latter category. He literally rolled out of bed, and the limp in his leg was very pronounced.

A few hours later, I watched as Nathan popped more pills into his mouth, his hands moving to his temples, rubbing them in a counter-clock-wise motion.

By two in the afternoon, he was on the third set of pain pills to numb the aches and migraine that plagued him. He had woken with a headache and it had increased as the day wore on. The medicine didn't seem to help, and he skipped lunch, opting to lie down in a dark empty office.

He stood and continued to limp, heading to the break room. It was so bad, that he was unable to walk it off.

Throughout the day, I observed him as he wiggled in his chair and readjusted himself in an attempt to find a comfortable position. He'd give up, sighing in defeat, and settled for whatever position he found to be the most tolerable.

It was easy to forget about his physical pain most of the time because he never showed the signs, but it was always there, lurking beneath the scars.

His hand swiped across the ribs on his left side in an unconscious attempt to soothe a sudden discomfort that flamed beneath.

There had been five broken ribs on his left side.

He helped me count them one day while exploring his body. He never shied away from my touch, but stared at me with a curious expression as I traced my hand around the long line of raised skin. Odd shaped scars left as evidence of his ribs cracking and breaking through the skin. I could feel them then, the places where bone had grown to mend the ribs back together.

I then took hold of his hand and guided it to the ribs on my left side. My hand pressed his fingers into my skin as I counted off where the four ribs my stepbrother had broken when I was younger were.

After work, we went straight up to his condo. He didn't speak as he guided me into the bedroom, or as we stripped out of our suits. Not even when he pulled back the comforter and crawled in, his eyes beckoning me forth.

His arms wrapped around me, his head on my chest. My fingers ran through his hair, brushing the strands away from his face. He sighed and snuggled his head in further before his body relaxed.

I hoped the next day would be better because it hurt to see him in so much pain and discomfort when I knew there was nothing I could do to help.

<br>

──────◆◆◆◆◆◆◆──────

<br>

We had a luncheon scheduled a few weeks later that consisted of Andrew, Benjamin, two clients, Nathan and I. It was to discuss the takeover of a smaller company and all the legality that would go into it.

We met at a nice restaurant downtown, and they sat us back in a private room. I was thankful to not be sitting between Andrew and Nathan, who were unhappy enough to be in the same room together, but hid from the client. Instead, Nathan had maneuvered it so I was sitting next to him in the large round table, with Benjamin on the other side. It seemed he liked Benjamin and his devotion to his wife, Marianne. Was it because it made him a non-threat in Nathan's possessive eyes?

Our salads arrived, but before I could even pick up my fork, I felt a hot hand on my thigh. It took everything in me to stop from jumping. I looked around to see if anyone had noticed, but everyone seemed to be too engrossed with the plate of veggies in front of them. I relaxed and felt the tingling sensation of Nathan's hand on my leg, gripping tight. Once he seemed satisfied no one was paying attention, his fingers began a circular motion on my skin.

I tried to concentrate on my salad, but it was difficult with him touching me. I stifled a moan while taking a bite as his hand moved up, reaching the hem of my skirt.

With slow, torturous movements, he roamed, leaving fire in his wake and an ache that was growing out of control. My hips flexed forward, shifting in my seat, trying to draw his hand down to where I needed him.

The wait staff cleared our salad plates and the conversation turned from getting to know one another to learning what the client needed.

No one noticed Nathan's missing hand, nor the nearness in which his chair was situated to mine, angled toward me. His hand pushed my skirt up farther while we waited for the main course, and I was thankful for the large table cloth that covered my lower half. He was just inches from the Promised Land. My thighs shook with need.

My face was hot, and I knew I was flushed scarlet due to his fingers stroking me through the thin material of my panties. I brought the glass of water to my lips right when Nathan's finger pushed the edge of my panties aside and slipped one finger in. I tried to swallow the water, but it became stuck when he entered me, and I began coughing and choking.

That gained everyone's attention, and five males turned to look at me. All the while, Nathan didn't stop, his fingers working slower, but deeper, sinking further.

"Are you okay?" Benjamin asked from my left.

"Yes, thank you, it just went down the wrong pipe." The looks of concern from the men at the table relaxed, and out of the corner of my eye, I could have sworn Nathan was smirking. "If you will all excuse me for a moment, I need to use the ladies room."

Being the gentlemen they were, the whole table stood as I exited the private room and made my way down the hall.

I located the ladies room and rushed in and shut the door, leaning against the cold tiled walls. After taking a moment to collect myself, I moved to the sink and turned on the water.

I was splashing some cold water on my face when I heard the door swish open. A hand grabbed me as I was drying my face off, and a second later, it had spun me around. My gasp of surprise was deadened by Nathan's lips on mine as he pulled my body flush to his.

"Baby, baby... Fuck," he whispered with a groan. His hand grabbed mine and moved it down, placing it over the rock hard length hidden beneath the fabric of his suit pants. "Feel what you fucking do to me."

I moaned, my lips searching out his while I rubbed and squeezed him. It earned me a growl, his eyes dark, showing the predatory sexual animal in him I desired.

"I need you. I need you now, or I'm never going to make it through the rest of this meeting without throwing you on the table and fucking you right there," he whispered into my ear.

I shivered at his words, my body igniting, moisture soaking my panties. He grabbed hold of me and we walked backward toward the wall.

"Nathan, we don't have time," I protested as he spun me around to face it.

He bit down on my neck. "We'd better be quick then."

His hand pressed on my back, and I leaned forward, my hands bracing against the wall. My legs spread while his hands moved under my skirt, pushing it up and over the curve of my ass. The sound of his belt coming undone echoed off the tile walls, followed by his zipper dropping.

His finger grasped onto my panties and pulled them down just enough to expose my throbbing wet pussy.

"Dripping for me already, baby? Such a fucking slut, you are." His voice was husky, making his dirty talk that much more powerful.

With a quick push, he slid between my folds and set up a lightning pace. I tried to remain quiet, which was always a difficult task whenever he was inside me. A few muffled mewls leaked out of my clenched lips. My hips pushed back against him, driving him deeper.

"Fuck. That's it, give it to me."

It took everything I had not to scream, but I couldn't keep it in when he slammed into me hard.

"You have to be quiet, little whore, or else they'll hear you and come in here. And I don't want them to interrupt my cock pounding your pussy. It feels too fucking good," he said with a moan. He hissed out a "fuck" when I tightened around him at his words. His hand moved from my hip to my mouth and he pushed two fingers in. "Suck."

I complied, my tongue working around the digits. I bit down when he found my sweet spot and continued to pound into it. My legs were shaking, my body tensing.

My mouth opened and my head tilted back, his fingers slipping from my lips. His hand then went to cover my mouth, stifling my cries as my walls clenched around him.

He continued to pound me, and I loved the feeling of my orgasm crashing around him, before he let go. The motions of his hips were erratic as he released inside of me, before stilling flush against my ass. He drew in a hard, ragged breath, the erotic sound causing me to moan.

He leaned forward, pressing his head against my back, one hand holding his weight against the wall. "Fuck, baby. That was…fucking great."

I let out a little laugh and shook my head. "You are so bad."

As my brain cleared, I realized the situation we were in.

*I'm fucking out of my mind and out of control…*

What was I thinking leaving the table? Of course he'd follow me; he was already fingering me before I'd left without any qualms even though we'd been in the middle of a business luncheon.

My head spun at the thought of getting caught in here with him.

How did he always make me forget everything that mattered to me—or used to matter?

My job was important to me, but Nathan meant more.

My chest clenched as I thought about what he meant to me.

"We need to get back out there," I reminded him since he was still behind me, bent over me, panting.

I needed to get my head back on straight and my panties as well. At least until the work day was over—then I could be what he needed, *do* what he needed.

After a moments rest, he pushed off the wall and removed himself from me. I whimpered at the loss, and he let out a little chuckle before leaning down and kissing the top of my head.

"Come on, Honeybear, we better get cleaned up real quick and get back out there before they send out a search party," he said.

I snorted at the way he made it sound like I hadn't just said the exact same thing, except without the nickname. He began zipping his pants back up, and I rolled my eyes.

It was amazing how he could go from brutal fucking one minute to lighthearted and silly the next. It was the Nathan no one else saw but me, and I reveled in that fact.

A smile spread from ear-to-ear as I straightened out my appearance. I evened out my breathing and smoothed my hair back in place.

A minute later, we were both inspecting ourselves in the mirror real quick to make sure we were presentable before attempting to sneak out of the bathroom. We walked back through the hall to the private room, and in the journey, I tried to make my legs behave, but I was still a little jelly-legged.

"There she is," Benjamin said with a smile. "And she found Nathan."

I smiled as I sat down, followed by Nathan. No one seemed to notice anything as I gazed around the table, until I reached Andrew's face. He wasn't looking at me, but considering there was food in front of him, it didn't surprise me.

But something seemed to be brewing behind his blue eyes.

"We sent Andrew out to find you two, but he came back empty handed," Benjamin said as he speared a piece of the pork chop in front of him.

I froze at Benjamin's revelation.

"I caught her coming out of the ladies room and dragged her outside with me for a minute," Nathan interjected, pulling me from my internal musings and coming up with something halfway plausible. "We had something we needed to discuss."

Andrew didn't say much for the remainder of the luncheon, or when we returned to the office. Even when he did speak, it was with effort and he wasn't smiling. I began to worry he had, indeed, heard us and what that might mean.

At the end of the day, we packed up, loaded into our respective vehicles and headed home. Nathan and I greeted Mike upon entering and stepped into the elevator together.

"You were a very bad boy today, Mr. Thorne. I don't know if I should let you in tonight," I teased, attempting to sound aloof once the elevator doors closed.

Out of the corner of my eye, I saw him smirk before turning to me. "Oh, really? And how are you going to manage that when I have a key?"

"Hmm, good point." Titling my head, I pondered how I could torture him. My index finger tapped against my lips. "I could deny you access."

His eyebrow quirked as he looked down at me. "Could you?"

"I think I could," I said trying to sound confident in my answer, but already knowing I would never deny him. I needed him more than he needed me; I needed his growing affections and the want that rolled off his body.

Leaning further over me and stepping closer, he had me pinned to the elevator wall, one of his hands on either side of my head. With his head next to mine, he whispered in my ear, teasing me. "Could you?"

His lips met mine and my mouth opened up to him. It took a few sparse seconds before our bodies were pressed together, arms pulling each other closer.

I fisted his hair and pulled his head back so his eyes met mine. "Could *you*?"

"Never," he admitted with panting breaths. "I could never deny you."

Somehow, I felt there was a double meaning to his words, but I didn't have time to ponder it because his lips were back on me, his tongue massaging mine. Our actions changed to a more desperate pace, and we were moaning while frantically trying to rid each other of our clothes.

The elevator signaled our arrival and we stumbled out of the carriage and straight into the wall on the opposite side. We were impatient as we attempted to disrobe each other. Hands and arms tangled with clothing and bags while we bumped against the walls on our journey down to my condo.

I somehow managed to get the top three buttons of his shirt undone, my tongue lapping at his skin, and was working on getting his suit jacket off, but couldn't get it past one shoulder. Nathan reached down and grabbed my thigh and brought it up to his hip. Unbalanced, we hopped backward until my back crashed into the wall where the hallway branched off to the different condos.

With my back braced against the wall, he picked up my other leg and pushed my skirt up my legs so he could nestle between my thighs. My legs locked around his waist and he pushed his hips forward, grinding his hard cock into my center.

He nipped down my jaw, panting and groaning. "You aren't going to walk straight when I'm done with you tonight."

I moaned and pushed my hips down against him. His teeth nipped at my neck while I continued my pursuit to rid him of his jacket.

"What the fucking shit is going on?" Andrew's voice roared from the end of the hall, grabbing our attention and making us stop as we turned our heads to look.

I stared at his tall figure in…surprise, horror, terror, shock? I couldn't decide which emotion, so I chose all.

Well, if Andrew didn't know before, he certainly knew now.

Nathan turned back to me, his head buried in my neck, hissing "fuck" over and over into my skin. His fingers dug into the flesh of my ass.

My face fell as my heart plummeted while I stared at Andrew. How could I have been so reckless? The whole day had been one bad judgment call after the other. We'd been so good, so careful, over the past few months, but it was obvious we'd slipped.

I'd never seen Andrew anywhere near as angry as he was in that moment; red faced, tense, seething, and shooting death glares at Nathan.

"I told you to fucking stay away from her!" he yelled. "And I told you to stay away from him!"

At that, Nathan released my thighs with a heavy sigh, and once my feet were seated on the ground, he let go of me completely. I was straightening my skirt and didn't notice Nathan had started down the hall toward Andrew. The muscles in his back were tense, and I chased after him in an attempt to diffuse the situation…or at least get us inside.

"What fucking right do you have to fucking say that to either of us?" Nathan questioned, staring Andrew down.

Andrew sneered while stepping forward and leaning over Nathan. "I can't fucking stand you. Now, get the fuck away from her."

Nathan's spine straightened, pushing him forward. "Make me. If she wants me to get away from her, she needs to do it, not some overgrown, jealous Neanderthal."

The situation was escalating, and I needed to get them out of the hall.

I pushed past them. "Boys, we need to get inside before my neighbor comes out, and you both know how she is."

I began searching for my keys, which ended up taking longer because I was going too fast. After a moment of not finding them, Nathan pushed his keys into my hand.

"Here."

Andrew gasped behind me, and I could imagine the look on his face.

I located the key and unlocked my door, ushering them both inside before handing Nathan back his keys.

"Are you kidding me? He has a fucking key? To your condo? Hell *no*," Andrew all but bellowed.

I slammed my bags down on the ground before shutting the door. "Andrew! You don't know anything about what is going on, so shut up."

"He's fucking playing with you, Lila. Open your eyes. He sticks his fucking dick in anything that has a pussy!"

At that, Nathan growled, and was standing inches in front of him.

If I thought I had seen an angry Nathan before, it didn't compare to the Nathan in front of me now. Every muscle was tightly coiled, his glare bone chilling.

His lips twitched as he snarled. "You don't know anything."

"How long have you been stringing her along? Making her think she's different from the other girls?" Andrew's posture mimicked Nathan's. I moved to pick up the glass vase from the entry table to protect it from being a casualty. In my mind, I was preparing to use all of my weight to force Andrew out the door to keep them from breaking out into a fist fight.

"As I said, you don't know *anything*. Because if you did, you would know the only woman I've been with for almost four months is Lila."

That revelation caught Andrew's attention. His head snapped in my direction, looking for confirmation. My arms were crossed over my chest, and I stared back at him. I hoped my expression was coming across as bored. Because that was how I was starting to feel about their little tiff.

His eyes grew wide and his head began shaking. "No. Him?" he questioned, his finger pointing at Nathan. "It was him at the bar? It's him who marks you? *Him* who understands you?"

I nodded, feeling that I didn't need to explain our actions to Andrew, especially when he was doing everything in his power to *not* listen to me.

"Yes. Me. I see her. I'm the one who sleeps with her every night. It's my cock shoved in that fucking tight pussy of hers. So, get the fuck out of here so I can pin her against the wall and make her forget that anyone other than me has ever been inside her."

I groaned. Nathan was baiting Andrew, igniting everything all over again. I stepped back when Andrew rushed forward, grabbing Nathan by his lapels.

"You don't deserve to be in the same fucking room as her."

Nathan pushed him off. "What the fuck is your problem? You just can't let her go, can you? Wasn't it you who left her? And what do you know about me, Andrew? That I fucked around with women over the last two years? Yes, that's true. I needed an outlet for my anger, frustration, and sexual needs. Who the fuck cares? She doesn't." His chin jerked over in my direction.

"If that's all you know and that's all you care to know, then leave," I told Andrew.

Andrew stared at me, ignoring my statement. "This is a breach of both of your employment contracts, you know that, right?"

"Of course we know. Are you planning on saying something so we'll both get fired? Is your prejudice of Nathan that great? So great you would endanger my job as well? And my happiness?"

"I… Lila…" He trailed off with a sigh. "I don't want to see you get hurt, and I think he could damage you."

"Nathan has no devious plan, no ulterior motives. He's a good man, and you need to open your eyes and see. Because all you're looking at is the act, what he shows you, not the real man. Now get the hell out of my home, and don't fucking come back until you're ready to know him—ready to know us. I'm an adult and can make my own goddamn decisions. I choose who I want to be with. And it's him. He's the one I want."

Andrew stared at me in wonder, a sad smile on his face. "Good girl."

I gave him a small smile in return, understanding the meaning between his two small words. I stood up to someone, against someone, and didn't retreat into my shell and take it. That's how strong I'd become.

He turned to leave when Nathan spoke, drawing his attention. "If you want to find out some truth – as true as the news will give you, anyway – then do what Caroline did: Google my name. And once you've done that and found some truth, then you can come and try to tell us what kind of person I am, but not before. Because I guarantee your opinions will change."

Andrew nodded, more sedate than when he arrived, and walked through the door, shutting it behind him.

I marveled that Nathan would share that with him. I still hadn't mustered the courage to look him up, but then again, I wanted the truth. I wanted to know the real horrors he'd been through. They wouldn't change my opinion of him; he was amazing.

Within seconds, I was back to being pinned against the wall, Nathan's lips on mine with hot and heavy desperate kisses. He pulled away before leaning in and nuzzling my nose. "Mine," he declared.

I smiled up at him, my hand moved to caress his cheek, my heart swelling. "Always."

# CHAPTER 23

The next morning, I was shocked into silence when Andrew walked straight up to Nathan in the parking lot and hugged him. Nathan hugged him back, and they exchanged what I could only describe as some secret, man-look. No fists, no angry words, but an understanding and friendship budded in front of my eyes as Andrew vowed to stay silent about us.

Over the next few days, they became lunch buddies, Andrew splitting between the two of us. It was almost like shared custody.

"Really?" I asked Nathan a few days later, my curiosity getting the better of me. I stood in front of the stove, a skillet full of ground turkey, springing the question on him as he walked back in from changing clothes.

"What?"

I waved the spatula in my hand. "You hug, exchange a look, and suddenly all of the animosity that's been boiling between you two for months is gone."

"That about sums it up."

"Men are strange creatures."

"Nothing had to be said. I told him to search; I knew what he was going to find."

"And what was that?"

He shrugged. "Half-truths buried in lies. Same as what Caroline found."

"And why is that?"

"Lila…"

"I'm sorry, I just…will you ever be able to tell me, or are you going to relegate me to the half-truths buried in lies as well?" The exasperation in my tone was evident.

He sighed and leaned back against the counter, his hands resting on the edge. "No. I don't want you to know that garbage. Don't do a search, please. I *will* tell you, I just…need to figure out how to do it."

"All right, okay," I conceded, not wanting to push him. "Please don't keep me waiting. I want to know you, all of you."

He stepped forward and wrapped his arms around my waist, pulling me toward him. He leaned down and kissed the side of my head before whispering in my ear. "I want you to know me too. And I will tell you, I promise."

I turned in his arms and tilted my face toward his, my lips pursing. He smirked down at me.

"Something you want, Honeybear?"

I made a fishy-face at him, cheeks sucked in and my pursed lips opening and closing. That improved his mood, a laugh springing from his chest before he too made fishy-lips at me and pressed them to mine.

I loved moments like that: sweet and tender. They were the times I was happiest, the times when Nathan was just Nathan, if only for a moment.

It was halfway through the next week when the relationship between Sadie and Will came out, no longer a rumor. We were all gathered in one of the large conference rooms, crammed in the small space, as Jack made the announcement that Sadie had submitted her resignation.

He informed everyone the policy was still in place, and Will would stay on since Sadie had resigned before action needed to be taken.

My mind began wondering what would happen in our case. I wanted to believe things would be fine, but I knew the reality of the situation. I surreptitiously looked toward Nathan; he was staring at the ground, mulling something over. Perhaps the same things that were on my mind.

"They're getting married next week," Andrew said next to me, his voice cutting into my internal ponderings. "Just a small civil ceremony. I talked with Will and he said Sadie's going to be a stay-at-home mom."

Stay-at-home mom. A foreign concept to me, but it made me wonder: would I ever be a stay-at-home mom? Would I ever marry and have children?

I shook my head. Yeah, right. Who would want to marry me? That was a pipe dream, something I would never obtain.

*No one wants you.*

*Why would anyone have you? You're worthless.*

I cringed at those words.

Without conscious thought, my eyes moved to Nathan. To my surprise, I found him looking back. I was unable to decipher the strange look on his face due to Jack's voice booming out that he had another announcement, drawing my attention away from Nathan.

He introduced us to the new hire, fresh out of law school, and she looked like she was going to fit right in with the Boob-Squad.

*Great, another one to fight off.*

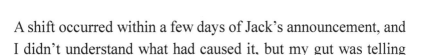

A shift occurred within a few days of Jack's announcement, and I didn't understand what had caused it, but my gut was telling me that things were changing.

Nathan had been…off for days. It was subtle at first, and then one morning it became glaringly obvious.

He had become withdrawn, and wasn't talking as much. He was short with everyone, including me.

It wasn't only at the office, it happened at home as well. He wouldn't look me in the eyes, and when he did, I saw either sadness mixed with a little disdain, or he would attack me sexually, his need so great at that moment that he couldn't hold off. But even in his moments of need, there was a wall forming.

232

After a few days of that behavior, I was awoken by screaming.

Blood curdling screams of pain and agony ripped out of Nathan.

I shook him, calling out his name to wake him. His eyes snapped open and he threw the covers back. His leg was stiff from sleep and it caused him to stumble on his way to the bathroom. I chased after him and found him leaning over the sink, splashing cold water on his face.

I was staring at him in the mirror, willing him to lift his eyes, but he wouldn't.

I called out his name, stepping toward him, my hand reaching out for him, but my call was ignored.

He toweled off his face before heading back into the bedroom and crawling back into bed. He walked right past me, shied away from my outstretched hand, and retreated, shutting me out.

Things deteriorated from there.

I'd overheard Shelia ordering that month's birthday cake, listing off who would be celebrating that month. Nathan's was mentioned, and I put it on my calendar, thinking about what to get him. A few days before the date, I asked if he wanted to do anything special. I was shocked by the expression on his face: vacant and bone-chilling.

"Please don't say that again, and don't tell anyone. I don't celebrate my birthday…not anymore."

It was such an odd thing to say, but I let it drop because something inside told me to stay silent. A knot formed in the pit of my stomach, and it was an eerie reminder of a time long before. His birthday passed. I couldn't even wish him a happy birthday. All I was able to give him was my body, letting him take anything he wanted that night.

It was two days after that when Nathan left early. It was odd, strange for him to leave, let alone in the middle of the morning and without saying anything to me. So, at just after five, I found myself fidgeting with my keys as the elevator ascended the fifteen stories to his condo.

"Nathan?" I called, my voice echoing around the empty walls as I entered.

A warm breeze guided me to the balcony off the living room. I stepped out into the warm summer air, my gaze searching for him. I found him sitting at the end of one of the lounge chairs. The sleeves of his charcoal grey shirt were folded up to his elbows, a beer bottle at his feet and a cigarette in his hand as he leaned forward, his forearms resting on his knees. His hair was a windblown mess, and his eyes were red.

"Nathan?" I called out to him again. There was no response; he didn't even look at me.

My mind began running wild with questions and theories. Was he fired? Did someone find out? No, he wouldn't have reacted that way if such was the case.

A glint of gold reflected in the sunlight and I searched for the source. Something twirled within the fingers of his left hand. My eyes focused in on a small band of gold, forged into a perfectly round circle.

A wedding band.

I stopped breathing, my chest constricting as the pieces came together. I stood transfixed on the metal as it spun in the light.

His wedding ring.

The thought repeated in my mind as the pieces locked in place. Whatever happened that marred his body, had also marred his heart. His wife had died. That had to be it. That was why he was damaged.

"You shouldn't have come today, Lila," he stated, his voice low and void of emotion, his eyes cast out onto the view of the cityscape as he picked up the beer and took a swig. "I can't control what I may do. I'll hurt you; I don't want to hurt you."

I pushed him for the first time. "I'm not going anywhere. Tell me, what's wrong."

He whispered so low that I almost missed it. "Four years ago today everything fell to ruin. Leave, Lila."

My heart sped, threatening to burst from my chest as his mood from the last week and a half started to make sense. "I'm not leaving, not when you're finally talking." I stepped closer to him.

He still didn't look up at me. "I don't just mean today. Leave me. What we have is fucked up."

"It may be fucked up, but it's helping us both. We need each other."

"I'm not good to be around."

"You are. You *are* good to be around." My voice broke.

In a flash, he stood and spun his arm around, releasing the bottle. It crashed into the brick wall, sending droplets of beer and shards of glass everywhere. I jumped back, surprised by his reaction. This anger was different, more potent.

"You don't fucking get it! I lost *everything* that mattered most. My family. The family they stole from me, and the one I pushed away for their own safety."

In two steps, he was on top of me, lips to mine, heated and desperate. His hands were fisted in my hair, pulling me closer.

"Leave me," he pleaded, pulling back with tears in his eyes. "I can't lose you the same way I lost her."

"I'm here, take solace in me. I need you."

He growled and walked me backward and into the wall. "I can't fucking *do* this to you; I won't," he said, but his hands held my arms on either side of my body, the brick biting into my skin, his body pressed tight against my own. He leaned down, his lips capturing mine, his tongue lapping as he attempted to devour me.

I tried to tell him it was okay, that I wanted it, but I couldn't speak with how crazed he was.

He released my lips. "Push me away and leave. Please, Lila!" His hands let mine go and grabbed my hips. With rough hands he dragged my shirt up and over my head. "I don't want to break you."

I couldn't do what he asked. I wanted to take him in and let him see that everything was all right, that I was there for him.

Manic hands moved back to my waist, his fingers digging in, his passion and desperation increasing. He was clawing at the clasp on my suit pants before he moved to pick me up by my ass and walked us back inside.

He was hard against my stomach. The vibration of the groan that came out as he set me down, and my body ran down his length, sent an electric fire through me. He released me long enough to tug his own shirt over his head.

He picked me up again and once we reached the bedroom, we fell onto the bed, his hands grabbing at me, unable to stay in one place. His lips were everywhere, his tongue lapping at any flesh he could find. He latched onto the waist of my pants, his mouth never leaving my breast, and pulled the zipper down before removing them along with my panties. He removed his own pants as well and was on me again, his hands using more force than usual.

He hovered over me for a small second as he lined up. I looked into his eyes and gasped at the nothingness I saw in them. The lights were on, but I couldn't find Nathan inside their depths.

He pushed inside and I arched while I cried out in pleasure. My body welcomed him, my hips rocking up to his.

I wanted to help him, but the situation was rapidly spiraling out of control. Everything was harder than usual, and every time he pulled out and slammed back in, it increased.

It didn't take long before I was screaming out his name as I came, my body reacting to his, the same as always.

His grip grew tighter, kisses rougher, thrusts harder. It was to the point of pain. Everything was coming to a head; Nathan was breaking.

He was ending us in the same way we began, but harder. Ripping apart our connection with force. His anger, hurt, and pain laid bare as he took it all out on me.

"Please, Nathan. Come back to me," I cried out, but I knew it was useless. I couldn't pull him out, he was too far gone.

I grabbed his head, a gasp forced out of me at his eyes; blank and glazed over.

My blood ran ice-cold. His eyes always held a fire when he was with me, but it was gone.

He was dangerous, dark and scaring me. I whimpered another soft plea for him to look at me, and come back. My palms stroked his chest as tears threatened to leak out of my eyes.

His hands tightened around my arms, squeezing so hard I cried out in pain. He was shaking, tearless sobs rocking his body.

He kept his mouth away from my neck and shoulder; he wasn't going to mark me.

This was it. The end.

A tear slid down my cheek.

His grip was harsh, bruising. His nails dug in deep at my hips, much stronger and harder than ever before. I tried to pull away, the pain intensifying, but I couldn't and he was too far gone to notice.

I couldn't fault him for it. I had asked for what was happening. I had let the beast inside of him out, allowed him to be fully unleashed upon me.

My muscles went lax, and I gave in to the sensations, unfolded myself so his needs could be sated and the nightmare could end.

The tears of anguish, both physical and emotional, poured from my eyes. I could feel it, his fingers so tight on my flesh. It was too great. We would not survive his pain, survive the night.

I shouldn't have come.

Words from the past came crashing down on me.

*It's your fault. You shouldn't have provoked him.*

I laid beneath him, tears streaming down my face. Hoping, praying, he would return to me. His muscles tensed, and I felt him empty inside me, collapsing on top of me.

After he had regained somewhat-normal breathing, his head rose from my chest. I could hardly see; my eyes were slits as I fought for consciousness. But it was enough for me to see recognition return to his eyes, followed by shock, then overwhelming sadness before I passed out.

I awoke sometime later in my familiar bed. It was neither comfortable nor warm, it was cold and empty. Just like I was.

He wasn't there, and I didn't need to call out to know for certain. His side of the bed lacked body heat.

Gone.

A shiver ran through me. I moved to sit up, but my body cried out in protest, and I looked down to find handprint-shaped bruises blossoming on my arms. There was a stinging sensation on my waist where I found crescent shaped gouges from his nails, along with more bruising and dried blood from where he'd broken skin.

There were other yellow spots forming on my flesh. I sighed and swung my legs over the edge of the bed. I stood up, my legs wobbling, and I stumbled, swaying back into the bed.

A piece of paper crinkled beneath my hand, and I looked down to find Nathan's handwriting across the page.

Lila,

I can't do this any longer. I refuse to hurt you again. Please keep your distance, and I promise I won't come to you anymore. We'll act like we never happened.

Nathan

I read and reread the words on the page, though I had already known. His mind was made up.

He left me.

Weak. You're weak.

Stupid. You actually believed he had feelings for you?

I stopped breathing, my chest felt as if it was being ripped apart from the inside. The pain was excruciating, doubling me over.

I wasn't strong enough. Strong enough to fix him, strong enough to heal him, strong enough for myself, or strong enough to hold us together.

Another wave of pain lanced through my chest.

Oh…this is what a heart breaking feels like.

All the walls I had built to hold the crushing dark abyss gave way, trapping me in its suffocating black depth. I was sent spiraling into the dark, the light fading, my strength gone.

I wasn't strong enough.

I wasn't enough.

Never enough.

# CHAPTER 24

Days, minutes, weeks, years, hours.
I didn't know how much time had passed, nor did I care. It was peaceful in the black.

Voices called to me, whispered echoes surrounded me. I could make them out, if I concentrated. But I didn't want to concentrate. I wanted the peaceful black.

Most of their words were lost in the depth, mangled, but I could hear the murmurs all the same.

Caroline, Andrew...*and* Nathan.

I could make out the tenor more than the actual words. Nathan didn't say much, for which I was thankful, but I could hear Andrew; he was angry, screaming and cursing. Caroline was pleading.

I shook every time I heard Nathan. His voice threatened to pull me back.

I didn't want to go back. The calm darkness held the pain at bay. I didn't have to feel my heart shattering in there.

Though the pain came through anyway every time he spoke.

It wasn't often, but it was there. He stayed silent, and I couldn't help but wonder why he was there. Didn't he leave *me*? Break me? Wasn't that why I had resigned myself to the darkness?

More voices came, an urgent tone, unknown. I couldn't feel my body, but I could tell I was being moved.

More time passed and voices came and went. Some familiar, others not.

Dr. Morgenson? He was angry, yelling at someone.

No more Nathan. He was gone. I couldn't feel him anymore. He left.

A feminine voice, smooth like Nathan's, showed up at some unknown point. She didn't talk around me, or about me like the other unknown voices did, but she spoke *to* me. I couldn't make out most of her words, but I could tell they were sweet and encouraging. There was a hint of sorrow in her voice as she apologized, but I couldn't understand why this unknown woman would do something like that.

My chest tore a little more, and I slipped back deeper, away from the pain.

Darkness prevailed. Up, down, day, night; I didn't know any of those. But I did know I was safe. The pain, the loneliness, the worthlessness; it was all unable to touch me in my own black world.

Nathan didn't want me.

I rose again, something was pulling me. Not a voice. I couldn't quite tell, but it pulled me from the darkness, calling out to me. I could hear the beating.

*Ba-bump. Ba-bump. Ba-bump.*

No voices, no sounds, just the beating, calling to me, pulling at me.

There was nothing but the darkness and the beating. And it was constant, unrelenting.

*Ba-bump. Ba-bump. Ba-bump.*

*Nathan?*

It drew me closer to the surface, and I heard the voices again. They spoke medical terminology—gibberish to my ears.

*Ba-bump. Ba-bump. Ba-bump.*

It was so close. There in the darkness. *He* was so close.

I began to shake, fighting against his call. I knew it was him, only he pulled at me. He wasn't in the room, but he was close.

The unknown voices were still speaking, but I didn't understand them. I only heard him.

*Ba-bump. Ba-bump. Ba-bump.*

"...*ven Palmer.*"

One of the voices broke through, calling out the name of the man who helped to conceive me but would never be my father.

All sound stopped. A ringing filled my ears along with the voice.

*"Emergency contact. This paperwork is about thirteen years old, but it does say next of kin. Perhaps we should call him? He would want to know about his daughter's condition."*

*No. No. No. Please. You can't call him. Don't. No!*

I thought I had been screaming in my head, but before me were two wide eyed doctors, staring at me in shock.

I began to scream, begging them not to call him, thrashing in the bed, tears streaming down my face as I yanked on the tubes in my arms in an attempt to flee.

"What the hell is going on in here?" I heard Dr. Morgenson's voice ring out through my screaming. "Lila. Lila. Calm down!" He called out to me, his hands stroking at my hair.

"Please, please, Dr. Morgenson, don't let them call him. Please. He doesn't want me. No one wants me," I cried. "I can't listen to him tell me again that he hates me."

I trusted Dr. Morgenson. He knew my past; he had worked with me before and knew I had no one. That turning to my former family would be worse than death to me.

"Shh, no one is calling anyone, Lila. It's just you and me here now. You need to calm down before you make me give you a sedative, which I really don't want to do." His voice was soothing.

I made my body relax back into the bed, but my breathing was still labored, tears streaming out of my eyes uninhibited. It was then that everything came crashing down on me. The pain in my chest seared like a red hot poker. I stared up at the ceiling in an attempt to calm myself, but it didn't help. A sob ripped through my body, and I turned to the side, my body curling in on itself as sob after sob poured out.

"Not enough. I'm not enough. Not strong enough. Now... I'm nothing. Nothing. Just like they always said."

"Lila, I need you to focus on me now, can you do that?" Dr. Morgenson asked.

I turned my head to look at him. He was blurry through the tears, but I could make out his black hair and the look of concern on his face.

"How do you feel?"

"L-like there's a h-hole in my chest. It h-hurts so much," I stammered, gasping for air.

244

"Breathe, Lila. You need to calm down. Take a deep breath," he instructed.

I complied as best I could. It was difficult with all the things I was suddenly feeling.

There was a pinch on my arm and coldness slipping up my veins and then nothing. I ceased to be. The blackness took me. Thank God...

When I came to, an unknown amount of time later, Dr. Morgenson was there, waiting for me and waiting to explain what was going to happen.

"Lila, I had to sedate you. Do you understand why I did it?"

Yes, I knew why, but I couldn't bring myself to speak. It hurt too much, so I resorted to basic communication through facial expressions and head movements. I nodded and closed my eyes. I didn't want to see the disappointment in his eyes. Not his too. I would listen to anything he had to say, but I couldn't bear to see that look.

One of the things I loved about my doctor was how perceptive he was and how he seemed to believe in me. If it wasn't for him in the past, I wouldn't have made it. And here he was again, bandaging me up so I could pretend to exist enough until...what? Until I decided I was done. Until I left and found something better or...

"Here's the plan. I'm giving you a new prescription. You're going to take it exactly as I prescribe it. And if you're still having insomnia you need to start taking the sleeping pills in conjunction. You will go to bed at ten p.m. each night. You will get up at six and shower, get dressed, eat something and go to work. I want to see you every Friday after work at six p.m. No drinking, no bars. Friends are allowed to see you, but only if they're supportive of you and don't interfere with your therapy."

I swallowed hard. What friends? Caroline? Andrew? Would they even want to be around me when I was a black hole of a being? I didn't care. What would I say anyway?

"If you agree and sign the release paperwork, then you can go home afterward. Any questions?" he asked, patting my arm.

He was being firm but also empathetic, and I didn't deserve it. Any of it.

"How long?" I asked in a whisper of a breath so I didn't crack in half from the pain.

He knew what I meant, and gave me a sympathetic smile before dealing my fate. "Indefinitely. You'll be on the medication until we get you going with some serious trauma therapy. This episode, this 'parataxic distortion' you experienced, it will come back. It always does until it's dealt with. But with how fragile you are right now, we have to wait until you can handle it because it will dig at your core and bring up all sorts of nasty memories you've suppressed and buried for years."

*Just say it...say the word... Broken. A step away from being institutionalized.*

But he didn't. There was no way I could come up with a better plan, and I was scared to do the trauma work. I'd avoided it in the past with him, because I didn't want to go that deep... because I knew I couldn't survive it. So, I did what I always did. I nodded my head like a good little girl, swallowed my terror, signed a damn paper and went on my way.

When signing my release, I looked at the date on the form and was stunned to see it was Saturday. It didn't seem like that much time had passed to me. Hours, maybe, but in actuality it was a little over three days.

Dr. Morgenson called me a cab after he gave me my personal belongings, and I stepped back into the ninth circle of hell: my condo. An empty inferno where I would suffer alone.

Two days without Nathan, and I had nothing but my pain to keep me company…at least until Monday, when I returned to work and entered a whole other, deeper level of hell.

⟶ ⟫⟩◉⟨⟪ ⟵

The pills did their job, though I didn't end up needing the sleeping pills. Sleep was something my mind begged for so I could shut out the pain. I didn't dream much, for which I was thankful. The other pills kept my mind groggy, and I felt like I was sleepwalking through the day.

It didn't take it all away. It only dulled the edges of the sharp stabbing pain. Now it was a general ache, a dull throbbing sensation as I zombie-walked through existence.

I parked in my regular spot, noticing Nathan's car was also in his normal spot. Creatures of habit. My breathing was even, the medication wouldn't allow me to hyperventilate, but it didn't stop my mind from dreading what I would see in Nathan's eyes. Rejection. Absolute repugnance at a woman who was not worth talking to, not worth thinking about, not worth having in his life. Only worth fucking until he was done.

Now he was done. He got what he needed, what he wanted, and we were over. I was expendable. I would have to go back to what I knew, fading away into the background.

247

With quiet steps, I walked into the confined space I'd shared with Nathan over the past five months. It was with great trepidation that I placed one foot in front of the other and moved forward. My eyes avoided his desk as I sat down at my own.

I turned on my computer and put away my purse. I didn't look at him, didn't speak to him, and tried to ignore his presence entirely.

A difficult task because I could still smell him and, per usual, he smelled divine. No medication could block that out.

I wanted to drown myself in liquor every night, but I knew it would make things worse. If things got worse Andrew and Caroline would tell Dr. Morgenson and he'd have me committed faster than I could blink.

However, if I remained lucid enough, I would still be allowed outside, could still work. I'd be left alone. At work I could still see him.

"Good morning, Delilah," he said in a whisper.

I cringed against his words and ignored them, turning my attention to anything that wasn't related to him.

Nathan didn't blink or move, but he breathed. In and out. So did I…only just.

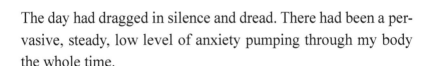

The day had dragged in silence and dread. There had been a pervasive, steady, low level of anxiety pumping through my body the whole time.

If Nathan had been stressed, it hadn't shown at all; he was hidden deep within himself, behind the blank expression he wore.

He left at precisely five o'clock with a small "good night," and I wondered if that was how it would be from then on.

I waited a few extra minutes until he was out of the vicinity before I gathered up my belongings and prepared to leave. It was one thing to see him at his desk, it was another to watch him leave, knowing he would not be going home with me. That was too hard to watch.

"You leaving?" Andrew called to me from the door.

"Yeah," I managed to choke out, my focus returning to the trivial task at hand.

"Lila, I'm glad you're back." He didn't mention what he knew about my situation, my hospitalization. I wasn't even sure he knew Nathan had left me.

One look in Andrew's eyes told me he knew it all, but he knew how much it would destroy me to hear him talk about it, so he stuck to safe subjects like dinner.

"Want to go get something to eat?" he asked, being the sweetheart he was.

I shook my head. "No. I'm tired. I'm going to go home and crash."

A look of concern crossed his face. "Will you text me when you get home?"

"Drew." There was a hint of annoyance in my tone. He was big-brothering me, but I had to admit that deep down I liked it on some level. It was a sign someone gave a shit about me, even if Nathan didn't.

When did my world begin to revolve around Nathan? I'm sure Dr. Morgenson would have something to say about that.

"Just humor me," he said with a genuine, caring smile.

Why? Why did he care? He didn't understand me, not really. No one did. Only Nathan, and he didn't want what he saw.

"Okay," I agreed, not sure if I was lying to him or not.

I'd deal with that when I got home.

"Caroline told me to tell you she's going to call you tonight, too. She had to leave work early today."

I grunted something unintelligible, shifted in my chair as I grabbed my belongings.

"Night."

The drive home was drab, but familiar, so I survived without any additional pain. It wasn't until I stepped through the door of my condo and looked around at the barrenness, that I choked.

I ran to my room and tore off my clothes. On my way to the living room, I stopped by the guest bedroom where I had been sleeping, and pulled off the blanket and a pillow. I refused to sleep in my bed. It smelled of him, and I didn't have it in me to change the sheets.

I crashed on the couch, grabbed my phone and pulled up Andrew's name to text him and let him know I was home safe.

I flipped through the channels before settling on a horror flick. It didn't take long before my mind shut down, and I welcomed the emptiness that came with sleep.

# CHAPTER 25

I was having trouble concentrating on the document in front of me and decided perhaps a cup of coffee was in order. The smell of the coffee would help to override the permeating scent of Nathan.

The hair-raising, cackling sound of the Boob-Squad's laughter could be heard before I made it into the break room. I didn't want to see them right then, but the need for coffee prevailed. I wasn't in the mood to put up with them.

"Oh, hi, Delilah," Jennifer said as I entered.

I walked up to the cabinet and pulled out a clean cup. "Morning, Jennifer."

There were four of them standing around. I couldn't help thinking they should be working.

"So glad to see you finally decided to return to work."

All of the sudden, I felt like I was in high school, being ganged up on by the popular girls. The difference was there was no stepbrother named Adam to lead them like when I was younger, just a warped sense of entitlement.

Ignoring them, I poured the liquid into a cup. My hand reached for the creamer, but it was blocked by Tiffany.

She refused to step aside. "I can't believe you left Nathan to do all of your work. Do you have any idea how swamped he was? He worked like a dog all day and then left, to sleep."

I sighed and pushed a strand of loose hair behind my ear.

"We offered to help, but he was too nice to accept it," Jennifer said. "He knows what his responsibilities are and doesn't go gallivanting around for days"

At that I laughed. It was almost maniacal, but I already knew I wasn't mentally stable anymore, so I paid no attention to it. They all stared at me.

*Yup, I've gone insane. Fuck you.*

"I'm so sorry to hear he was having such trouble handling things for three days while I was hospitalized," I said, sneering at them all. "Your concern is touching as were your offers to help. Amazing, isn't it, that I did it all by myself for over four months and not once did any of you even attempt to assist me or see if *I* was okay. *Huh.*"

My hand flicked, spilling the coffee all over the counter, splashing onto Tiffany, before pushing past them and back out the door. I stormed back into the office and sat down. I heard Nathan make a sound like he was about to speak, but then changed his mind. I didn't look at him or try to find out what he wanted. I didn't give a damn what he thought anymore . I couldn't afford to. The cost was too high.

252

The combination of my outburst and Nathan's mood kept the Boob-Squad away from our office for the remainder of the week. It was in the rare instances that they actually did need help, that they would brave an entrance into our cave. Not only had the mountains returned and we were drowning in work, but Nathan was not being his usual friendly self as well. He wasn't being off-putting either, though. He was just...there.

A ploy so he could ignore me easier, at least that was what I thought.

———————

I'd been back a few days when Jack Holloway called me into his office. Upon entering, I found it vacant, so I waited for his return. I perused his bookshelves, admiring the collection, when my eyes landed on a photo frame.

I picked it up off the shelf and stared at the photo it held. It was Jack; his arm was around a woman in her twenties. She was tall with blonde hair past her shoulders and blue eyes. Plain, but beautiful all at the same time.

"My daughter," Jack spoke from next to me. I hadn't even heard him enter the room, let alone walk up to me.

"She's beautiful," I replied.

"Yes, she was," he said, taking the frame from me. A look of longing and sadness filled his eyes, and I felt guilty for bringing her up. "Grace...passed away a few years ago."

I felt awful that I'd forgotten. "I'm sorry."

He gave me a small smile. "Thank you."

He returned the frame back to its rightful place. "Delilah, please sit." He directed me to take a seat in one of the leather chairs in front of his large mahogany desk. "I called you in because I'm concerned. I don't mean to pry, but something or someone put you into a catatonic state last week. Since then your attitude has soured."

"I'm sorry, Sir, I don't mean to be disruptive."

"That isn't why I called you in here. I'm worried about you. While your work has remained in its stellar state, I worry about your health; mental and physical. I'd like to suggest, and I only mean this as a suggestion, that you see a therapist. I know of a great one—"

"I already have a therapist," I said, interrupting him. "I just haven't been to see him in a while."

"Might I suggest giving him a call? You've been with me for five years, and I've never seen you like this." He looked at me like he actually cared, and then he said words that made my chest clench. "You know you're safe here. Protected. I care about all of my employees, and I make sure they're comfortable at work."

There was something about the way he'd said I was safe. It made me wonder just how much Jack Holloway knew of the truth.

"Please, know I'm here for you if you need anything, Delilah."

⟫⟫•◗◗⟫•⟪

The week had been difficult.

Get up, go to work, maybe eat lunch, go home, crawl into bed, rinse and repeat.

I never ate dinner anymore, so it didn't surprise me that after a week, my clothes were starting to fit a little loose. Not falling off me, but it was easier to button my tailored suits than it had been.

I didn't care. I stopped caring. Caring took too much effort and caring for someone took everything.

Andrew, Caroline, and Ian had begun referring to him as "the asshat." They didn't talk about him much, which was okay because I didn't want to talk about him or talk at all.

So I stopped.

No more talking.

No more smiling, no more caring, no more mask.

No more Lila.

I was existing, not living.

I didn't put on an act anymore, it took too much effort. Perhaps this was the real me, exposed for all to see.

Thursday afternoon, we were so behind with work, that later in that afternoon, I realized I hadn't eaten anything that day. I found myself making stupid mistakes and knew I needed to take a break, but at the same time there were only two hours left until I headed out.

Jack had dictated I wasn't to stay past six for the next week or he would escort me out personally. Any attempts to tell him I was fine fell on deaf ears. He was the boss after all.

Nathan hadn't spoken to me since I had returned, but today he felt the need to address that I existed.

Nathan broke the silence when I was midway through the Hansen file. "Delilah, go eat something." In my peripheral, I could see that his head had not turned in my direction; he was still staring at the screen.

"No," I responded, my eyes still fixated on my monitor, my fingers typing away on the Hansen file.

"Go," he commanded.

"I'm not hungry." Didn't he realize he couldn't tell me what to do anymore? He lost that right.

He slammed his hands down on his desk, startling me. My head snapped up, and I watched him walk out the door at a brisk pace. He returned a moment later and threw something hard onto my desk.

"Eat it."

"No."

"Eat the fucking granola bar before I shove it down your throat."

I picked it up and threw it against the wall. It hit with a crack, and then fell to the floor.

"Oh, I've heard that threat before," I spat at him.

His eyes grew wide as he stared down at me. His disinterested act slipped and I could see, just for a split second, the pain beneath.

I had to admit, it hurt to see that tortured look in his eyes, because if he felt like that, I couldn't help but wonder why he had separated us. All it brought was a tight stab in my chest and hope.

I had to squash the hope. Nothing good came of it.

Hope wasn't allowed in my bleak world, along with asshats and their granola bars. They took too much energy.

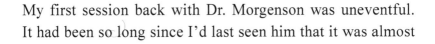

My first session back with Dr. Morgenson was uneventful. It had been so long since I'd last seen him that it was almost like we were starting from scratch. He already knew about my past, so there was no need to delve into those sordid details.

The present however…well that was a brand new beast.

He made me talk about Nathan.

I didn't want to talk about Nathan, but Dr. Morgenson wasn't letting the subject drop entirely. He was a tricky one.

"So, tell me about the last few months," he said, his gaze expectant.

I went into the story of Nathan coming to work at Holloway and Holloway; a few choked sobs tried to escape at the mere mention of his name. I didn't want to talk about it, I wasn't ready, so I turned myself off before I broke down again, and slipped a neutral expression back on. Dr. Morgenson knew it as well because he cleared his throat, uncrossed his legs and leaned forward, staring me straight in the eyes.

I sat unfeeling, uncaring, pretending not to give a shit about my life as he probed into my emotional state.

"Go on…" he encouraged.

"And then I slipped. I became comfortable in what I knew was a volatile relationship." What else was there to say?

"I want to help you get better, Lila. I need you to know and accept that there are people who care about you. People you can trust," Dr. Morgenson stressed.

I knew that was the case. I knew I could trust him, but what was the point?

The session ended and I left; the first of many I would attend over what felt like a millennia.

---

A crappy morning to add to my crappy week awaited me when I awoke. It was raining.

Couldn't I catch a break? Wasn't my life miserable enough from the beginning? Why then did he have to come into my life and make me believe there was something worth living for, only to take it all away?

Nothing. I was nothing. Just as they'd always said I was. I would never amount to anything. Yup, there I was, shell of a fucking human being because I fell in love.

*Love stinks. Worse than asshats…*

The windshield wipers moved back and forth at a furious pace as I waited in the left hand turning lane for an opening. The light was still green, stale red for the cross street.

Green means go, but it appeared not everyone knew that red meant stop.

I heard the squealing of the tires against the wet pavement. I saw in my peripheral as a work van flew over the white line before the crunching of metal filled my ears.

That was then it all disappeared. The pain…the dull ache in my heart, and Nathan, too.

All I knew was black and stillness…

Until I heard the sirens. Breathless voices and clamoring hands touched me.

It was later when a voice broke out above all other sounds, screaming, "Oh, God. Lila! Love, no! No! Get your fucking hands off me. That's my girlfriend! Lila!" That was when I knew I was probably about to die.

Only angels sounded like that—only my Nathan…

Turn the page
for an exclusive sneak peak of the second part
of the Breach Trilogy:
**Infraction**

# CHAPTER 1

I woke to throbbing pain throughout my body, a pounding headache, and the screaming of my name. It was faint, but growing in intensity as it moved toward me.

My eyes opened and I looked around, seeing the door of what I recognized as a hospital room.

"Lila! Lila!" Nathan's voice cried out. It was a frantic, panicked tone I had never heard before.

"Lila!"

"Mr. Thorne! You need to return to your room!" what I assumed was a nurse screeched at him.

"Lila!"

"Don't pull that out," another voice scolded.

"Lila!" he wailed, and it sounded like he was on the verge of tears.

It was clear he was ignoring the nurses as his search for me continued; they were threatening to call security.

"Lila!" he called out again, desperation flooding his tone. He was louder, only one room away.

My chest tightened, and my heart began beating at a furious pace.

Seconds later, his hands appeared on the doorway, bracing himself while his eyes searched for me.

I gasped when I took in his appearance; he was wearing nothing but a hospital gown. One tube hung from his wrist, hanging down on the ground.

His expression was what had me in shock and my heart wrenching. Tears streamed down his pink cheeks; his eyes were wide and frantic, a look of despair overpowering all other emotions.

As soon as his eyes met mine, his body relaxed, and his face morphed into one of relief and joy.

"Lila!" he cried out once more, stumbling toward me.

He reached out and grasped onto the sides of my face, his forehead leaning onto my bandaged one.

"Oh, thank God. Thank God, you're alive."

Warm tears landed on my cheeks as he continued mumbling. I stared at him in stunned silence. This was not the Nathan I knew. The mask was gone, and for the first time I was seeing the true Nathan without any inhibitions. He was raw and lay bare before me.

I didn't move, I didn't speak, I just laid there stunned. He was crying.

Nathan was crying.

34652516R00153

Made in the USA
Lexington, KY
14 August 2014